TYCHE'S CRUSADE

A SPACE OPERA ADVENTURE EPIC

EZEROC WARS
BOOK 9

RICHARD PARRY

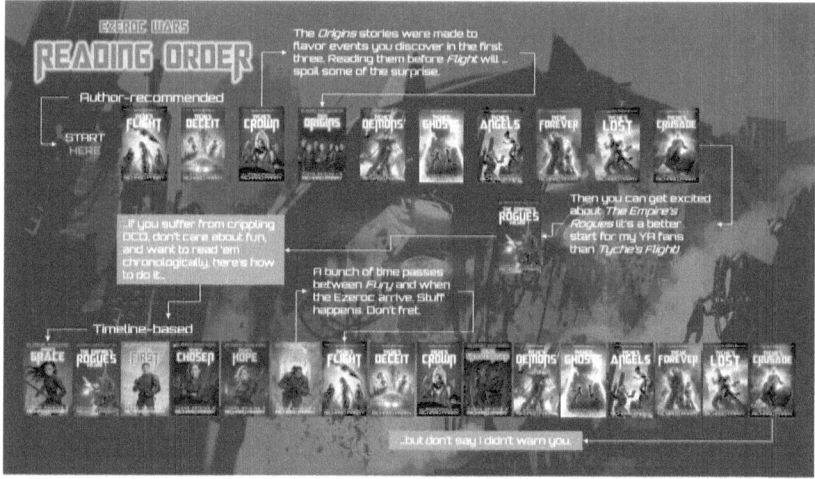

TYCHE'S CRUSADE

FREEDOM BRINGS THE EMPIRE TO ITS KNEES.

Pastor Cleaver and his Church promise life eternal to the faithful. His offer is simple: join me, and live without pain or fear.

Behind the pulpit, the Ezeroc wait. Their gospel is corruption. Their mission: bend the Empire's will and turn its weapons against the throne.

The order is clear—**kill the Emperor and Empress.**

Nathan Chevell stands between humanity and oblivion. With an aging heavy lifter and a worn-thin crew, he must stop a monster hiding behind the power of an empire.

The enemies are closing in. The odds are impossible. And this time, **Nate's famous luck may have finally run dry**.

Tyche's Crusade is the explosive final book in Richard Parry's *Ezeroc Wars* series. If you love page-turning space opera with razor-sharp dialogue, desperate stakes, and the fight for humanity's soul, grab your copy today!

YOU'RE AWESOME

You could have picked any book, but you chose this one. That means a lot.

Your support keeps independent authors like me forging ahead, writing the stories we love (and hopefully, the ones you love too). Whether you're here for the characters, the worldbuilding, or just a little escapism, thank you for being part of this journey.

You. Kick. Ass.

ROLL FOR NARRATIVE

WHERE WORLDBUILDING AND
OVERTHINKING COLLIDE

Love stories that linger in your brain long after The End? Ever wonder why some books hit like a natural 20 and others critically fail their way into the 1-star abyss?

Join *Roll for Narrative*, my hub for sci-fi and fantasy lovers. I explore storytelling like a rogue casing a dungeon, review movies, books, and games, and dish out writing tips like a chaotic-good bard with a grudge against bad prose. No spam, just good stuff.

Join the quest:
https://rollfornarrative.parrydox.com

In ten minutes, you'll face the most powerful enemy since forever. Chin up.

Nate held onto his acceleration couch's straps like they'd save him from drowning in a sea of emotions. The dropship was full of *anxiety/ready* and *fear/focus*. The feelings rattled against him like pebbles thrown against glass. They came from the men and women with him. Many he didn't know, and knew he'd never get a chance to on account of them dying below. A few he'd seen in the halls of the *Mercenary*, and one or two he'd shared a drink with.

The dropship wasn't built for carrying cargo other than brave souls. Forty Marines shared the trip with the Emperor and Empress. Another six dropships shared their approach vector. Across Earth, the Navy deployed similar ships against Church outposts on the basis you couldn't be too careful. Their forces were spread thin, but Nate's future-sense said it wouldn't matter. The real battle would be here, in San Francisco, in just under ten minutes.

Grace sat in a couch beside him, her face calm. Relaxed, even. He wished he shared her serenity, and certainty that all would be well.

GRACE *I don't think all will be okay, I think it'll be better with you*

NATE *I prefer it when you lie to me*

She shifted on her acceleration couch. Nate had to admit, even sitting down she drew the eye. She didn't wear armor, leastways not the type the Marines wore. Her black synthetic clothing was form-fitting. The quartermaster said it'd turn the kiss of steel, maybe even take a kinetic round or two, but he couldn't guarantee it against blaster fire. Grace had nodded, saying, *I don't plan on getting hit anyway.*

Nate, never one to turn away a good ace up the sleeve, wore similar clothing underneath sensible armor. The Empire's falcon rode golden wings on his chest plate. The armor chafed some, but was light enough so's not to be bothersome. Gold winked at him from where his gloves didn't quite meet shirt. His metal arm reminded him not all stories had happy endings.

The dropship wasn't like his *Tyche*. Where his heavy lifter was comfortable, a home, this spacecraft was all business. It didn't even have a whiskey dispenser.

They'd launched from Navy ships in geosynchronous orbit above San Francisco. Their target was the Church of the Undying Dawn's main Chapel and Pastor Seth Cleaver. Intel said he was inside, waiting to be shucked like an oyster from its shell.

"Hard contact." The clipped voice came over the ship-wide comm, and belonged to Dennis Boat, an apt name for a Helm. The dropship weaved, leaving Nate's stomach back aways. He could imagine hands on sticks, steely eyes watching the ground, counter-measures turned to eleven as they headed for the dirt.

It wasn't a big deal. If the ground assault team hadn't taken out the air defenses, the trip would've been cut short already. *And seriously, what kind of church has AA cannons?* If there was ever confirmation that Cleaver was the enemy, this was it.

A holo set in the middle of the dropship bloomed to life. It updated with RADAR and LIDAR maps of the terrain, highlighting gun emplacements, the Church's Chapel, likely numbers of ground forces, and their fellow Marine transports. A dropship's beacon winked out, the craft torn from the sky by weapons below. Nate closed his eyes, thinking back to a time where he'd protected an Emperor, not play-acted as one. They'd been torn from the sky too, and it'd cost him an arm and a leg.

Grace's hand found his arm, her touch light but steady. "It'll be different this time."

"Hah. You're only saying that because you weren't there. This will be the same." Nate cranked a grin out of spare parts. "Or, it'll be different. We could die."

She laughed. "I think we should talk with Cleaver about who should do the dying."

"Rapid disembark in thirty seconds." The Helm's voice remained tense over ship-wide comm. Nate figured Dennis could learn a thing or two about calm under fire from El. Still, despite his anxiety the man did an admirable job of getting them to the deck without the dropship exploding.

The vessel's engine roar changed in pitch, climbing to a whine. The attitude of the deck shifted as the Helm brought the nose up, scrubbing airspeed through friction and use of Endless fields. Well before Nate thought thirty seconds had time to amble past, the dropship's wide doors opened, a ramp shooting out. Marines were already boots on metal, running for the dirt outside.

Nate released his harness, raising an eyebrow as Grace shot past and out. *How is it you're the only one still in here? Might be getting old.* He clanked across the deck, making the daylight outside. It was weak and grainy, struggling with the clouds and ever-present ash in the atmosphere.

Boat had the courtesy to point the dropship's ramp toward the Chapel. The building was huge, making the Winter Palace look like an exercise in modesty. It rose against the skyline, basalt and marble winking their contrast in the light. A massive double door waited beyond a faux hedge maze. The doors stood maybe twenty meters tall, large enough not even Kohl could persuade them open.

Hundreds of civilians fought Empire forces in gardens Nate figured had once been serene. They used blasters as readily as weapons of opportunity. He saw a woman swing a rake at a Marine, beside a man trying his level best to skewer a sergeant with the broken haft of a similar gardening tool.

Four other dropships sat to the left and right, their disgorged Marines making progress across manicured lawns. The blue-white flash of plasma fire spat across the space. Debris from a mortar explosion showered Nate with dirt, and debris nicked his face. He touched blood. *You and your ideals. You could have left this to others.*

"You could have left this to me!" Chad jogged past, offering a mocking half-bow and flourish as he went. The spymaster held a rapier at the ready, sidearm in his other hand.

Saveria followed in his wake. "You really should have. This leading from the front business will get you killed."

"I was ... stop reading my mind!" Nate drew his blaster, wondering what he meant to do with it. Barbecuing civilians didn't sit well with him, so he also drew his black blade. *Slightly less lethal, since you can disarm instead of skewer.* The sword felt heavy with intent in his right hand. The golden fingers of his left gripped his sidearm in readiness.

CHAD Wasn't reading your mind, you're predictable

SAVERIA Also, we told you so

Nate broke into a ragged run. He wasn't doing much leading from the front, what with all the waiting by the dropship. The smoke was too thick to see Grace in the melee, what with the visual noise of hundreds of people throwing themselves against the cheese grater of the Empire Navy.

Some good news in this sordid mess was there wouldn't be Ezeroc here. No roaches boiling up from the dirt. No flying insects with stingers, ready to inject larvae into a person. The nanotech plague worked *for* humanity now. Algernon bought that with Saveria's life.

A pair of frenzy-eyed churchgoers ran at Nate. One held a shovel, the other a blaster. The plasma weapon looked to be Navy standard issue, suggesting at least one of them knew how to kill Marines. Shovel-wielder was a short, stocky man who looked like he'd be more at home as a bartender. The woman holding the plasma carbine had the nervous disposition of a bomb maker. She steadied herself, pointed the weapon in Nate's general direction, and pulled the trigger.

Future-sense tapped Nate on the shoulder. *Step to the left three paces. Pause. Right two paces.*

Nate danced across the grass. Plasma chewed the space he'd occupied. The woman did a double-take, then glanced at her weapon as if it were to blame. Shovel-wielder reached Nate, taking a wild swing. Nate's sword caught the shovel on the blade, sliced through steel, and sent it spinning away. He slugged the man across the jaw with the butt of his sidearm. The should-be-an-innkeeper dropped to the dirt in a pile of unrealized potential.

He ran at the woman, blade low. *Dodge right. Stop. Duck.* Plasma scorched the air. Nate felt the deathly heat of it, the scent of ozone everywhere. He swung his sword, cutting the carbine through the barrel. The weapon sparked, its cartridge detonating in a bright flash. The woman screamed, tucking her burnt hands under her arms.

Nate offered her a nod, then hurried on. Ahead, he caught the gleam of steel as poetry, Grace's sword moving as a visible extension of her will. She ducked and weaved. Unable to see the future like him, she had to rely on skill. Nate was honest enough to admit he'd rather be lucky than skilled, but Grace had the knack of making skill look desirable.

He joined her in a moment of calm. Smoke chased leaves across the grass, an eddy of wind tousling Grace's hair. The double doors of the Chapel remained closed. He pointed with his sword. "We need to get in there."

She nodded. "It's lucky we brought a bottle opener. Sergeant!"

Grace turned to a stocky woman who looked manufactured from granite and salt. "We need that door open."

"Aye." The sergeant, a woman who wore the name Hudnall like a combat boot, clicked her comm, bawling orders. Nate caught *ordinance* and *of course there's no hurry, it's only the Empress.* "Your Highness, might be a good time to take cover."

Grace nodded but didn't move. A Marine jogged up, youth and enthusiasm in every motion, a long tubular weapon in hand. He offered Grace a quick smile, shy like he was in the presence of his idol, but shut it down because he was a *Marine*, for heaven's sake. "One bottle opener, as requested."

Sergeant Hudnall glared. "You're not getting paid overtime, Coles!"

Coles gave a curt nod, dropped to one knee, and raised his launcher. Sighting down the barrel, he paused for a two-count, then pulled the trigger.

A contrail of brilliant fire shot from the weapon to the doors. They exploded in a shower of wood fragments and steel reinforcing. Nate ducked, metal arm up to shield his head, but nothing hit him. The blue crystal glimmer of Grace's mind-shield held before them, a bubble of safety protecting them and the two Marines. When the debris settled from *raining death and fury* to *there's a lot of smoke,* Nate nodded to Coles. "Nice work, Marine."

"My pleasure to kill the sworn enemies of the throne, sire." Coles winked at Hudnall, who swore, then darted back into the fray.

Hudnall watched him go, then turned her regard on Nate. "Anything else, sire?"

"One thing. Very important." Nate leaned close. "Try not to die. Or let anyone else die."

Her hard face softened. "It'd be my pleasure, sire."

Nate gave another nod, then headed toward the breached door. Grace loped at his side. "You always do that. Make them feel like they're the most valuable person in the world."

They arrived at the door. Flames still licked the wood. Smoke trickled toward the sky outside and the vaulted ceiling inside. "They're laying down their lives for us. That's a thing I can't look past."

"I wasn't criticizing. I was..." She trailed off, eyes wide as she took in the Chapel's interior. "Thankful. How is it that the Church has a Van Gogh?"

Nate stepped inside the Chapel. Or, Chapel anteroom, because despite this chamber being as large as a stadium, and something Guild Engineers would be proud to construct, it sported many doors leading to locales unknown. Around the interior lay countless *objets d'art*. The Van Gogh looked real to Nate's gutter-thief eye. A statue of David copy stood in a shaft of light from above. He squinted. *That may be the* real *David. What's an Ezeroc-infested person want with artwork?*

It caused a niggle of doubt. The Ezeroc didn't like art. They liked *food* and saw humanity as a movable feast. If Cleaver had this much art here, he either had a very good interior decorator, was into the collection as a means of wealth preservation, or... *Or, he's not Ezeroc.*

Nate shook his head. Saveria called the man *a new kind of Queen*. Chad, once he woke, agreed with her. They called Seth Cleaver a *threat to humanity*, not just the throne. Nate shrugged off his nagging thoughts, focusing on the mission ahead. They were here to end that threat. Intel said Seth Cleaver called this place home. Empire spies saw him here, walking about, sucking O_2, and passing benedictions.

Five meters inside, feet padding down carpeted steps so plush they needed a mow, Nate felt the stirring of unease. His future-sense cast about, finding no targets, but still sending fingers of cold fear up his back. Ten meters in, even Grace felt it, slowing to a halt, blade raised, head on a swivel. "What *is* that?"

"Future-sense," offered Nate. "Or, good ol' fashioned human dread. Here we are, in the den of a spider."

"Not that." She shook her head. "*That.*"

Nate cocked his head, listening. After a moment, he felt it. So faint you might think you'd missed it, a whisper right on the edge of hearing. It sounded like the hissing of sibilant Ezeroc speech, except... *Except there aren't any Ezeroc on Earth. Not anymore.*

He broke into a run. Grace kept pace beside him. A shout behind him brought him up short. "Sire!" Nate turned, taking in Hudnall and a clutch of Marines. "We still storming the gates?"

"Hold here, Sergeant. What's ahead isn't for you."

She hefted her rifle. "Nothing a little plasma won't cure."

They're so willing to throw their lives away for you. That's why the vote's important. They need to choose. "Hold *here*, Sergeant. No one comes through that door."

Hudnall searched his face, then gave a tight nod before turning to her Marines. "You heard the Emperor. Secure this position. I want clean lines of fire. I want it fast. And you, Coles, will secure that expression in the black depths of your heart before you get entrenching duty!"

Nate headed down the massive room. The sense of space was eerie. It felt as if they walked inside a cavern, a stone vault constructed above, not below the Earth.

"This feels like an Ezeroc burrow," Grace offered.

"I wish you wouldn't say what I'm thinking," Nate said. "It's not helping my calm."

"I was just saying, because—"

"Still not helping." Nate looked about, trying to find targets. There wasn't anyone in here. No guards. Not a single member of the faithful. Certainly no priests, or whatever the Church stocked in their stead. His sense of unease grew, rising to a crescendo as he felt the still waters of his mind ripple as someone — or some*thing* — nearby gathered their will. A powerful esper was at work here.

Grace made no comment, her lips pressed into a line. She would have felt it before him, stronger, and keener to her core. Her sword glinted from the lighting high above, but her black suit gave nothing back to the enemy's fortress.

"Where is everyone?" Nate turned a slow circle as they

approached a shallow stairway leading up a level. It was perhaps ten meters wide. The carpet was as plush as everywhere else, looking new. *San Francisco's still in ruins, but Cleaver's found materials and people to build himself a shiny new house.*

"At Mass." Grace shrugged. "I don't know. I'm not familiar with this religion."

"I'm glad you didn't say, 'preparing a trap.' Because that's what I was thinking." Nate swung his sword, getting the feel of it right in his hand.

"I didn't say that because you'd get anxious again."

"*Anxious?*"

"Or fretful." She sniffed, then pointed to the doors atop the stairs. "Whatever it is, it's in there."

Nate nodded. No more putting this off. He jogged to the steps, swearing a little at the excessive use of vertical space as he climbed, then shouldered the doors open. They didn't even have the decency to creak, sliding open on hinges so smooth the Guild would no doubt wonder how they worked.

Inside was a smaller room, but no less plush. At the far end was a throne, showing exactly what Seth Cleaver planned. *The man already has a Church to rule but has designs on all humanity.* It looked like the designer preferred the baroque styles, a tall back rising well above the natural level a human might need for good lumbar support. On the throne sat Cleaver himself.

He looked like he could stand in a hurricane and call the weather mild; his shoulders were wider than Kohl's, and fervor burned in his eyes like a searchlight. A Caesar cut kept brown hair squared away. He didn't smile, but Nate imagined straight pearly whites that could chew ceramicrete to powder. "Nathan Chevell." His voice was a melody to behold. Angels would weep to speak like that.

"No." *Naturally, he's a sending. The power we've felt? It's him projecting himself into this space. But he's so clear, so visible. Could Grace send so well?* Nate wandered inside, checking out the corners.

No guards, and no clergy. "It's *Emperor* Chevell. For a while longer, at least."

"My apologies." Cleaver smoothed a silk shirt, then stood. He was a titan, grazing the lofty heights of two meters. "What can the Church do for the Empire?"

Grace raised an eyebrow. "The Church? Nothing. We've no quarrel with people who want to believe in something bigger than themselves."

"What she means is, you're scum, and we're going to put you to the blade." Nate hefted his sword for emphasis, then shrugged, almost apologetic. "You know how it is."

"You wasted all these people to come here." Cleaver smiled, like a post-cream cat. "Yours and mine both. Mine went willing into the light, Emperor. Did yours?"

"Where are you?" Nate sheathed his blade, then looked at his blaster. *Probably won't be needing that either.* He holstered it. "I feel like this is anticlimactic. After Viukde, I expected a brief round of fisticuffs, then one of us bleeding our last on the dusty ground. I wanted to meet you, Pastor, and see what kind of creature figured to make me into a corpse."

"Earth isn't good for me right now." Cleaver cleared his throat, the sound apologetic.

"For your kind, hey?" Nate offered a smile, showing more teeth than strictly necessary.

Cleaver shrugged. "You're going to kill me without trial. Isn't it odd that you seek to end your only viable opponent in the election?"

"Not sure that was a part of my plan," admitted Nate. "I came to end the Ezeroc threat to our home."

"You've nothing to fear from me." Cleaver paced in front of the throne, like he needed to burn off a little of his brooding demeanor. "They're a cancer."

Grace laughed. "You *are* Ezeroc. You might be able to hide it from those without our gifts, but..." She shook her head. "You will not lead humanity into the darkness."

Cleaver looked astonished. As a person who'd inflicted more than his fair share of surprise on people, Nate figured the look for genuine. "I'm but a simple pastor."

"You're an agent of the enemy," Grace hissed. She tapped her head with two fingers. "I *remember* what you did to me. To *us*." She swept her arm in a savage arc, indicating *all of humanity*. "I know what you put in me. I'll *release* you, Seth Cleaver."

"Thing is," Nate injected himself into the conversation like he'd never left, "records say you were on Viukde. Head of a mission, before leaving with a powerful wind in your sails. Middling at sermons and such before, yet now you have this."

"I've been blessed." Cleaver's teeth showed like a shark.

"Fair enough." Nate turned to Grace. "Do you know where he is?"

She closed her eyes for a moment, then shook her head. "He's not close. If he was blood of my blood, I might be able to... From the strength of his sending, he's in-system."

Cleaver nodded. "I'm not hiding, Empress. We'll meet when the time's right." He snapped out like a candle on the wind, vanishing without even a puff of smoke.

Nate turned toward the doors, feeling weary. *It never ends.* "Best we find out where he's gone."

Grace nodded, then pointed to a cam above the throne. "Why do you suppose the good pastor has surveillance in his sanctum?"

"I can think of several bad reasons, and no good ones." Nate sighed. "He wasn't on Earth because the nanobot swarm still holds the line. He *looked* human, but maybe it's only skin deep. Would the nanites kill him?"

Grace looked away. "Algernon might know."

"Time we go ask him." Nate strode for the door. "While we're about it, let's get Kohl sober. I've got a job for him."

ONE

When the cap said he had a job, Kohl figured it for a nice easy evening of thuggery. Were it so simple. When Nate went *full* Emperor on him, holding out Kohl's Captain of the Black uniform, he wondered who'd died.

The answer, it turned out, was *no one, yet*. Nate demanded answers, all while feeding Kohl anti-hangover medication. The one ray of sunshine in the whole experiencing was when Nate said, *I need you to get intelligence, because my spymaster sucks*, and Chad looked sour, like someone stole all his apples.

It was almost worth putting the uniform on for.

But he did it anyway, because talking Nate around when he was like this was a thing a post-hangover Kohl had little patience for. After he'd got out of the cap's sight, he'd headed for his quarters, stripped the uniform off, and put on his street threads. Nate wanted the whereabouts of Cleaver, and Kohl wouldn't get that looking like the long arm of the law. Where information like that pooled tended to be at a lower water level, the kind of place sewage settled into after it was done dirtying up the streets. While Kohl didn't mind a fight, the places he'd be going tonight would view the uniform as a kind of challenge, and he'd be uncomfortably outnumbered.

At least the hangover meds were working.

Pants on below a mostly-clean shirt, Kohl chose boots that looked purpose-built for stomping faces. On the way out of his quarters, he snared his new laser carbine. It was much like his old one, except Hope said this one would work better. He completed his image with a sidearm, then shrugged his way into an armor vest. No sense in being an idiot about combat.

Kohl palmed the door controls and stepped into the corridor outside. His room was below the usual bright-lights-and-happy-smiles levels of the palace. It used to be a store room, and in a way it was again, because it held Kohl and his weapons. It made him hard to track down, aside from those in the know. One such knowledgeable person waited outside, all gleaming gold. "Al.",

"Hello, October." The construct straightened from his lounging against the wall. "Where are we going tonight?"

"'We're' not going anywhere. *You're* staying here, and *I'm* going to find out what Dizzy knows." Kohl figured that was the end of the conversation, charting a course toward the cargo elevator at the end of the hallway.

Al kept pace easy enough. "I believe you're likely to get yourself killed. Much as I enjoy the festive air of funerals, the Empire needs you in top shape. Chad advised things are likely to get 'real.'"

"Chad said that?" Kohl hammered the cargo lift's controls. It clanked somewhere in the shaft above, then began its descent. "That's not very specific for a man in charge of information."

"I suspect his attention is focused on other matters."

"He's getting laid." Kohl rubbed the back of his head. "Makes one of us."

"Jealousy ill becomes you."

"I ain't jealous. What he and Ellen do is between them. I got coin I could divert into non-drinking activities. 'Cept, I need thinking time." The elevator arrived, door sliding wide. The interior wasn't dark or dirty. This was the palace, after all. It was big, used to carrying loaders and crates and Guild machinery. He stepped inside.

"You said thinking, but meant drinking."

"Same thing." Kohl eyed Al as he slipped into the elevator beside him.

The construct bounced on the balls of his feet, eagerness vibrating off him. He looked ready to rumble, even with that new silver arm of his. "Why are we talking to Dizzy? I thought he was a purveyor of broken starships."

"Selling broken starships don't pay the bills." Kohl selected a level at random, leaning against a wall as the car jerked into motion. "Dizzy's a hawker of more valuable things."

"Information." Al nodded. "So, you're going to see Dizzy and beat the information out of him."

"Exactly." The car stopped, doors sliding open. Al stepped out. Kohl palmed the door controls closed after him, catching the machine's bright-white stare before they were cut off. *No sense in letting Al see the softer side of you.*

He pressed another button, more carefully chosen this time. The car resumed motion, heading skyward. Above was the palace garage, replete with vehicles that'd take Kohl close enough to the slums for things to get interesting. He wouldn't get so close as to get shot down, though.

After a minute, the car settled on the garage level, doors opening to reveal a cornucopia of sights and sounds. People scurried to and fro, loading or fueling air cars, dropships, and lifters. A wide yawning door led to the open air outside, some hundred meters above the ground. Racks of ordnance stood in orderly rows, harried Engineers moving about and speaking soothing words to machines in need of care.

Back against an air car stood Al, like he'd been there waiting awhile. "Hello again, October. Shall we go?"

Kohl stormed from the elevator. "You shouldn't come this time."

"Nonsense," Al said. "I've prepared this vehicle for our use."

Kohl eyed the air car. It was robust in an unflattering way, but more importantly, flew without the Empire's falcon. Didn't look armored, but he wasn't fixing to shoot at or be shot by Dizzy. It'd do. "Fair enough. Get in."

———

SAN FRANCISCO'S night skyline was aglow, life returning as Hope, by way of her Guild, worked her magic. Almost everywhere had power, and where they didn't, portable generators served the city's needs.

One dark smudge on the ground marked the slums. It had less power than most parts, on account of those with an entrepreneurial spirit stealing the deployed generators.

Al piloted the air car, because Kohl didn't want to. "I like adventures," the machine admitted.

"I hope you like boring nights too. There." Kohl pointed at a barren square of dirt where building foundations struggled from the ground like broken teeth. "That'll do."

Al guided the machine down, settling into the ruins. The doors winged open, and Kohl stepped into the night air. It smelled of smoke, more here than elsewhere, because this part of the city was hammered harder than others in the war. Also, people burned tires for fun in these parts.

He headed away from the vehicle. A group of four men rushed him from the shadows. They'd seen the air car, no doubt figuring on helping themselves. Kohl didn't slow, winding his arm back and clotheslining the first with a swing. The man's feet left the ground, arriving almost at his head height with the force of the strike, before landing with the rest of him on the dirt. He groaned.

The other three came to an abrupt stop. Kohl lifted the asshole on the ground up, dusted him off, and said, "I will pay you a huge amount of coin to make sure this air car is here when I get back."

"You what?" The clotheslined man looked in decent shape, a little anemic maybe, like he could use a burger and fries.

"Here." Kohl held out a handful of good Empire coin. "More when I get back." He sauntered into the night, Al's golden form jogging after.

"October." The machine's voice was hesitant. "You didn't kill those men."

"That's right. Life's hard enough on those down here without losing your father, or brother." Kohl adjusted his carbine's sling, making sure it was ready for an easy grab. "They're just hungry, is all."

"What if they take your coins *and* the air car?"

"Nate's got plenty of cars," said Kohl. "He won't miss that one."

"And if they're still about when we return?" Al cast a glance back at the four men.

Kohl followed his stare. The wannabe thugs milled about, turning coins over in their hands, and looking confused. "I'll give 'em more coin. I've no need of it."

"You're not into charity."

"I'm into *recruiting*, Al. We're about to go balls-deep into a new war. One against bigger assholes than last time." Kohl hawked dirty phlegm onto the ceramicrete sidewalk. "I want people who will fight."

"Because they're desperate and hungry?"

"Because they want to fucken *win*." Kohl shook his head. "No place for a losing side in what's coming next. Second place on the podium means becoming food for the roaches."

Dizzy's establishment was four more blocks up. The area's quality descended as they progressed. Watching eyes followed them. Even Kohl's non-uniformed appearance was moneyed enough to draw interest, but Al stole the show. Constructs didn't come here often, and when they did, they weren't made of gold.

The slums were rife with a danger economy. Men and women worked the streets, plying their bodies for coin. Others stole, or tried to, because there wasn't much worth taking. A burned-out building held what smelled like a copper whiskey establishment, but Kohl knew it wasn't moonshine you'd want to drink. You'd quaff it to keep warm, hoping the whiskey blanket didn't kill you on the way.

No one tried to mug them again. Kohl was almost disappointed, because the last encounter hadn't worked him up enough. Kimberly was always on at him about the importance of a good warm-up, and he figured on a little more action in the next hour.

Dizzy's place was designed to be difficult to find. The small hustler kept himself off the grid. The main entrance was at the end of a warren of corrugated metal lean-tos. At one time they probably housed the desperate and needy, but the gentrification effect of Dizzy's business shuffled 'em on. All that was left was dirt, broken ceramicrete, and the faint smell of stale sweat curling between metal walls.

Kohl squinted at the sky above. It was dark, the moon unable to peer through the ever-present ash cloud glaring over San Francisco. He didn't mind the darkness. If people didn't see what he was about, it meant he wouldn't have so much explaining to do.

"Where are we going?" Algernon stepped around a pile of rubble pinning a plastic bag fluttering in vain for freedom.

"We're going to a fight club." A sheet of metal rested like the others, but Kohl's practiced eye spotted holes cut so a man could grunt it aside.

"You came here to fight?"

"No, I came here so *you* could fight." Kohl grabbed the metal, gritted his teeth, and heaved. It moved about a centimeter. "Here. You try."

Blink, blink. "You want me to fight?" Algernon gleamed as he grabbed the sheet of metal. One golden hand, one silver. He picked up the wall segment like it was a sheet of cardboard, dropping it to the side with a *clang*.

Kohl winced as he watched Al swivel. *If I tried that, I'd be in traction for a month.* "It's what's gonna happen." Behind the panel was a more-or-less round hole in a brick wall, a maw of soft gums leading to a stone throat. Down the tunnel, warm yellow light hinted at things of promise. "Huh."

Algernon raised a gleaming golden finger. "I don't condone bloodsports."

"It's fine." Kohl adjusted his belt. "Not going to be very blood-sportlike, on account of you being a machine." He headed into the tunnel, ducking a little to get through the wall. Whoever busted the hole hadn't figured on their clientele being plus-sized. Maybe there was a separate fighter's entrance?

The tunnel opened out into a corridor, winding across a cerami-crete floor. Five meters in, they turned a corner and found the first dead guy. He appeared, even in death, a man with whom you wouldn't want to fuck. Light combat armor, big arms, and tattoos over his face. They weren't the glowing shit the kids of today got, but old-style ink like Gracie's dragon. Kohl squatted beside the body. The dead guy's chest was concave, like he'd been hit by a train. The face ink looked gang-related, some of it recent work. "Might be there's a land-grab down here. New muscle, working old streets."

"He's still warm." Al turned away. "Dead fifteen or twenty minutes."

"He's still armed, too." Kohl checked the fallen man's weapon. It was a stubby kinetic weapon, printed from a fabricator, but new enough. He ejected the magazine. "Still got plenty of rounds in here."

"He shot an armored foe." Al bent, silver fingers finding a fallen bullet. "Here."

Kohl took the bullet. The normally rounded nose was squashed. A quick check found another four spent bullets. *Quick burst of fire against a shielded enemy. One that busted in his chest and kept on walking without taking his gun.* "Construct."

"My people don't war with yours."

"Maybe ain't your people." Kohl brushed his hands, then stood. "Betting odds on you just went down, though. If there's another construct here, it could be an even fight."

"Hah." Blink, blink. "Oh, you're serious. Don't be alarmed, October. There are no others like me left. I'm the last of my kind. A butterfly, unable to mate. The last bird to hear my own song. A lone dinosaur—"

"I get it." Kohl lumbered on.

"Perhaps you should go."

Kohl ground to a halt. "Why the hell would I do that?"

"Because a construct will make short work of you." Al spread his hands. "I don't mean to cause offense, but you're," he looked Kohl up and down, "*meat.*"

"Yeah? One of my meat buddies is in here." Kohl pressed on, reaching a doorway. A big metal door was on the ground beyond, the surface deformed where something very strong punched it free from its hinges. The ground was scraped where metal feet found purchase. The landing beyond the door led down wide steps to a big area, in the middle of which was a fight cage. Inside the cage was nothing but body parts.

Outside the cage, also body parts. Lots of what could've been moneyed folk were in pieces. Kohl drew his attention back to his immediate surrounds, because right beside the door were three more guards, all down.

One was still alive. Big, ugly, bald dude. He took in Kohl, then looked past him to Al, gave a whimper, and tried to crawl away. This didn't go so well on account of him missing an arm, the ragged bloody tatters of a stump leaving red streaks on the dusty floor.

Kohl stepped in before the guy could drag himself down the steps and maybe hurt himself more. He crouched, grabbing the guy's belt and hauling him back. The asshole tried to fight, but all he managed to do was get blood on Kohl's arms. "Hey." Kohl gave him a shake for emphasis. "Hey! What happened?"

"You did." Ugly's eyes found Al again. "You and your kind."

"Ah." Algernon crouched beside Kohl. "Another construct?"

"Yeah." The ugly guy faded. Kohl sighed, removing a stim from his combat harness. He jabbed Ugly with it. The stim hissed, and after three seconds, the guy jerked, eyes wide. "I feel—"

"You feel high on life, I get it." Kohl slapped the side of his face. "Stay with me. A construct came in here, and did all this? Why?"

"Not another construct. *Him*." The man pointed with his bloody stump at Al. "I'd remember those eyes anywhere."

"He's clearly delusional. All meat socks are prone to massive perception errors." Al stood, scanning the room. "Wait here." He went down the steps.

Kohl turned back to Ugly. "Was the construct covered in synthskin?"

"No." A shake of the head, feeble despite the stim. "It was *him*. Gold. We know the Emperor's pet machine. Didn't figure on having to fight him."

The pieces didn't fit, leastways because Al'd been with Kohl all the parts of the night that mattered. "A *golden* construct came here?"

Ugly nodded. "There's only one."

"Did the construct have two golden arms? Or one silver, one gold?" Kohl jabbed a finger in Al's general direction without looking.

Ugly, now well on the way to dying, turned his head. "Silver?" He slumped further onto the cold ceramicrete. "I don't know."

Kohl stood. "Fuck this. Where's Dizzy?"

"Done. Took him." Ugly sighed, but it was mostly air escaping a body like rats leaving a sinking ship. "Am I gonna die?"

"Probably." Kohl tapped his comm, flagging a request for a medtech and a cleanup crew. He didn't know if his Empire clearance would get much, but it was worth the effort. The big, ugly, bald asshole wasn't dead, hadn't run away, and was generally useful by way of both giving information and not crying about it. Patch him up, and he might make a good recruit. "What's your name?"

"Does it matter?"

"Not today, but it might tomorrow."

The ghost of a smile lit Ugly's lips. "Then tomorrow, you'll have it."

"Fuck," Kohl offered, with a hint of irritation, but it was lost on Ugly. The fallen man slipped into unconsciousness. It wasn't pretty like in the holos. One minute there was something behind those eyes, the next his body sagged, chest barely rising with the body's will to suck O2. No more answers there, so it was time to root through the garbage.

THE FIGHT CAGE was about what you'd expect if you'd been in one, which Kohl had. The wire walls brought back memories from a long time ago, when he'd been one of the people making up the grime between the cracks.

He'd had his face pressed against mesh just like the stuff here, while someone worked him over. Kohl shook his head. *That was a long time ago.*

The cage was about ten meters across. The mesh stretched all the way to the ceiling, fifteen meters above. The lighting up there wasn't amazing, but he could make out handholds and chains up there. An enterprising fighter might scale the walls, either for escape or tactical advantage, and rain death from above.

Inside the cage was an abattoir. There wasn't enough intact meat to work out how many people were fighting when shit got real. Remnants of clothes were strewn about, fabric alongside leather, all of it looking red and wet. No armor. No weapons. Wouldn't be much fun being stuck in a cage with Al, that's for sure, and Kohl figured whoever came in here didn't have the golden man's sunny disposition.

Al sidled on up, like he was cautious about poking the bear. He waited to Kohl's left. Kohl gave him a glare. "Spit it out."

"The blood flow in your face tells a story."

"It says I need more cardio?"

Al shook his head. "Perhaps you should go. Let me finish this."

Kohl grunted, turning away from the cage. "This was finished before we got here. We need to find Dizzy."

"Because he's a friend?" Al's bright-white eyes scanned the room, doing what was probably the thirtieth pass for clues.

"Because he knows things. The little fuck has fingers in all the pies. This," Kohl swept his arm, taking in the room at large, "is how a little weasel like him finds intel. Get a bunch of moneyed folk down here. Free drinks," he pointed at a row of dispensers against a wall, "and sit back and listen for news."

"There are no recording devices here." Al shrugged. "I've looked."

"Course not. Bad for business." Kohl rubbed his nose. "Dizzy's crew are in the crowd. 'Cept, they're in *pieces* now." He sighed. "Fuck *all* this."

Al stepped closer. "Come, October. We'll find your friend." The machine's eyes brightened. "The good news is we have a trail to follow."

"Bloody footprints?"

"Better. I thought about what your colleague atop the stairs said. Another golden man, like me. It makes no sense, because I'm," he pressed his silver hand to his golden chest, "the last of my kind."

Kohl scratched his head. "You going somewhere with this?"

"What if I'm *not* the last of my kind?" Al held up a finger. "Don't interrupt."

"I wasn't—"

"Interrupting," Al said. "I've hijacked the city's surveillance network. There are many black spots, particularly around here. A dead end, but it got me thinking. Do you remember when I almost died?"

"This on Mercury, or the other time above Earth?" Kohl took a step toward the machine. "You know what? I reckon you should just tell me, on account of Dizzy being in the hands of bloodthirsty criminals."

"Ah, of course." Al's eyes dimmed for a second. "I don't get many opportunities to showcase my talents."

"You mean, to show off."

Al steamed on like he hadn't heard. "Above Earth, in the last major battle, shrapnel penetrated my armor. Hope Baedeker provided her rig as a power source. Post that event she supplied me with a new tritium battery."

"A what?" Kohl nudged his toe through something red and wet, uncovering an Empire coin. *They didn't steal anything. Just killed everyone and did it quick.*

"An atomic energy source. Mine was very old and didn't work well. An old tritium battery is likely to have errors. Leaks. A whiff of background radiation we can follow."

Kohl looked about. "There was a leaky reactor in here?"

"Focus, October." Al clapped his hands, metal chiming. "There is a trail we can follow. I believe the meat sock breathing out his last by the door was partially correct. While I wasn't here, someone like me was. Do you know what this means?"

"We can find Dizzy?"

"It means I'm not the last of my kind." Al's eyes glowed like tiny stars. "I'm not alone."

THE STREETS out the back of Dizzy's fight club looked much like the ones at the front. People were furtive. Lighting was bad. Nothing of value lay anywhere in reach.

Al steamed on ahead, ignoring all. He acted like a hound on a scent, eyes front, pace quick enough to force a jog out of Kohl to keep up. The buildings about them still held despair close like an old addict friend. Fires burned in barrels, but the flames didn't make Kohl feel warm. It wasn't the thought of following a stray radiation leak. There'd been plenty of rads in Kohl's life. Part of starfaring life. You took your pills and the problem went away.

Al had it in his head the end of this particular rainbow held a pot of gold. Gold in the shape of a man or woman, just like him. Except they wouldn't be, because Al was decent, if a little slow on the uptake. The construct who'd entered Dizzy's place was a psychopath. They'd milled an entire room of people into gruel.

And maybe it was fair enough. Bloodsport audiences weren't the most nurturing kind of folks. Could be they deserved their fate, but...

But that motherfucker went above and beyond, didn't they? What was the term the constructs used before the cap brought 'em onside? Rendering.

A whole room of people were rendered to a thin slurry, but then the parts'd been wasted. Left to spoil. Kohl eyed Al's back as the golden man charged ahead. Golden, like the sun, honey, or treasure, but inside lay a crystal mind atop a heart of iron. Al was like them, in the ways that mattered, but his kind? Maybe not all of 'em were cut of the same cloth.

Al slowed as they approached a wide warehouse. It rose thirty meters from the dirty streets. The walls were constructed of big ceramicrete blocks. It looked intact. All the windows were in place. A little graffiti spoiled the aesthetic some, as did a huddle of assholes out front. Kohl counted five. They wore robes, or maybe the right term was cassocks, but held carbines, which spoiled the holier-than-though look a little.

All the assholes turned, perhaps warned by their god, but more likely because Al was a shining gold beacon with glowing eyes. All five froze for a moment, like they'd seen a ghost. *Which is probably close to the truth, on account of another golden man doing the rounds.* One looked to start making a fuss. "Hold!"

"Hello, meat sock!" Al called.

The speaker did a double-take. "Meat what?"

Al strode forward. "We're here on a matter of some importance. You're holding a man of less than ordinary stature, about so high," his silver hand jabbed out below Kohl's shoulder height, "who we'd like to speak with in relation to Empire interests."

Cassock scrabbled for his carbine. The weapon danced tantalizingly out of reach, probably because churching didn't provide the same skillset as soldiering, but the intent was clear. Kohl unlimbered his carbine. He shouldered it in a smooth motion, the laser targeting system giving a whine. Red light painted the cassocked asshole, then his body ruptured in soupy gore. A wet splattering sound accompanied the pieces of him raining to the ground.

Al let his hand fall, glancing at Kohl. "I haven't asked them about the other construct."

"I'll save you one." Kohl moved the barrel of his carbine to cover a woman who'd managed to get her weapon up and pointed in their general direction. It *whine-chunked*, her body spraying backward in a shower of superheated water and meat. The wall behind her shone red and wet.

One made to run, so Kohl shot him next. *Three down.* Of the two left, one aimed a weapon at Al, the device roaring as he fired. *Kinetic weapon.* Bullets *pinged* off Al's chassis. The golden man looked at his chest, then turned white eyes on his enemy. "Hold, frail human!" The man kept firing, so Al bent, picking up a stone. When he leaned forward, bullets kept coming, which made Kohl hotfoot it behind a barrel. He risked a peek, seeing Al take aim with a stone. The construct tossed it, the rock passing through his attacker's head with the sound of a dropped watermelon. Al turned to Kohl. "What on Earth are you doing back there?"

Kohl adjusted his carbine, then leaned further out. He pointed the weapon at the final man's legs, pulling the trigger. The laser carbine *whine-chunked*, the man's leg disappearing into red mist, associated cassock parts blazing into floating carbon. He screamed and fell to the ground, rifle clattering against the rubble-strewn ceramicrete. "Your problem is you don't understand people."

"I understand you perfectly." Al brushed himself off. "You take on challenges you shouldn't, without numbers on your side. You do it often, and this is the result." He pointed to the four dead people and one now-crying man.

Kohl worked through that. "I guess we're kinda dumb that way." He headed for the mewling asshole on the ground. He grabbed the front of the guy's cassock, hauling him up. *Feels pretty light, but I guess missing legs will do that to you.* "Where's Dizzy?"

"Who?"

"I have a better question." Al arrived beside Kohl. "Where is my counterpart?"

The man, whose eyes were shining with fear, panic, dread, or a sickly amalgam of all three, settled on Al. "Gone."

"Gone where?" Kohl gave him another shake.

The ground trembled. The rumble of a titan clearing their throat shook the air. Kohl spun to the warehouse. Through the windows, orange and white light glowed, before roiling flame blew the glass outward. Kohl ducked, glass showering around them. It sprayed across Al's metal form, but any noise it made was lost in the thunderous roar of a starship's main drives building pillars of fire.

From the top of the warehouse, a starship nosed for the heavens. Kohl wanted to say, *you don't launch a starship without blast walls,* or, *who the hell's flying that thing?* He settled for turning, making for a line of ramshackle metal at a run. He dragged the cassocked, one-legged asshole with him.

Skidding around the metal, flames on his heels, he figured this for the end. The metal wall was thick steel. It looked harvested from a dropship. Maybe a drive cowl, even. It'd take the fire but could just as easy blow away while doing so. Kohl cast about for a solution. The air felt oppressive with heat so intense it dried out his eyes and made his tongue rasp across his lips. The air hazed with it, a presence like death shouldering toward him on waves of fire.

Al rounded the wall, his body shimmering with heat. The machine punched his hands into the metal shelter, any clang lost in the raging inferno of a starship launch. Al held onto it, his perfect golden form reflecting the light of flame cascading around the edge of their little sanctuary.

The force of the flames drove the wall back, and one of the

construct's feet slipped. Kohl dropped the cassocked asshole, barging forward. He braced the wall alongside Al. He knew he wasn't as strong as the machine, but he wasn't going to die without standing shoulder to shoulder with his friend.

Kohl's gloves smoked against the metal. He could feel the burning heat through them. The steel and ceramicrete sandwich of it shivered in a buffeting storm, then settled. The air stilled, but Kohl had trouble sucking it in. All the oxygen felt gone. He gasped, sliding to the ground as a starship raced for the heavens.

Al let the wall go, the big piece of metal falling away with the sound like the gong at heaven's gate. Around them, blackened buildings smoked. A tiny lee of unscorched ground lay about them. Kohl lay back, waiting for the air to be cool enough to not burn his throat, and full of enough O2 he wouldn't die.

The construct turned bright-white eyes on Kohl. They burned almost as bright as the starship's drives had. "He did this. Someone like *me* did *this*." A silver hand stretched out to the buildings about them. Screams came from the distance, but close there was nothing but the *tick-tick-tick* of cooling stone. "Everyone here is dead. Even their own, within the building they launched from. A starship can rise on Endless fields." The construct turned his eyes to the heavens. "Why?"

"Loose ends," Kohl rasped. He tried to rise, but his hands hurt where they touched the ground. Burned, most like.

Al took three steps to the robed asshole. He grabbed the man by the cassock, hauling him up and holding him at arm's length. Where his golden hand touched cloth, fabric smoked from the heat. "Where?"

"I don't—"

"*WHERE ARE THEY GOING?*" Al's voice sounded loud as a megaphone.

The man looked away. Kohl didn't know what he saw in the construct's face, but it sure as hell wasn't mercy. "Mercury."

Al let the man fall, then moved to Kohl. "I can't pick you up. It will burn you."

"It's fine." Kohl put the barrel of his carbine against the ground, pushing himself upright. "Been standing on my own for long enough. Can do it a while longer." He took a couple wheezing breaths. "You okay?"

"No." The construct shook his head. "Mercury is my home. It's where my people are. And there's a new coordinator-class construct heading there. Do you know what that means?"

Kohl considered his carbine. "Means I'm gonna need a bigger gun."

TWO

Chad chose the cafe because no one went there. It had bad service, worse coffee, and the cakes on display were of questionable providence. The cafe's big desire factor was its location: it was on the second level of a megaplex. It had a balcony overlooking a massive outdoor area. Chad used the balcony to survey a vertical slice of humanity.

The outdoor area would have been, during happier times, the kind of grassy square people could take their families. Brave trees still struggled from the dirt. Their leaves would have an ashy residue like everything else, but because it was night, that detail was blessedly hidden. The square no longer held happy families. Hawkers vied with relief tents. Buildings stood vigil on the other three sides of the square, gentle guardians with faces made of massive vid screens. Entertainment shows gleamed in the night, but without sound.

"This place is perfect." Chad turned at Saveria's voice. She carried a tray with two cups of coffee and what *looked* like a collection of cakes. Chad retained his natural suspicion about the food. He'd eaten here before.

"I know, right?" Chad swung back to the vista of humanity. "It's perfect for getting the pulse of the people."

"I meant, this particular place. The bad coffee drives everyone away." She put the tray on a table, then ran fingers through her hair. "I can't always keep their voices out of my head."

"You get used to it." Chad hunched at the guard rail, peering down. "We still on for tonight?"

"Yes, but I'd like to once again raise what a terrible idea it is." She joined him at the rail, arms crossed. "Dating is weird enough without us double dating." Saveria looked out over the crowd. "Hope and I are, uh, new at this."

"You think the admiral and I know the rules?" Chad hooked thumbs into his belt.

"At least you're both people."

"So are you. Kinda." Chad tried a smile. "Like, ninety percent."

"I hope you die of the bad cancer." She settled at the table.

He watched as she took a sip. Her whole face puckered. "It's horrible, isn't it?"

"Is it even coffee?" Saveria put the cup down like it was an unexploded mine. "How do they keep this place open without customers?"

"It's coffee." Chad slid into the seat opposite her. "Big Tony Benedicto."

"The who now?" Saveria nibbled at a cake, making a face. "It *looks* good. Why doesn't it taste good? I feel cake's like pizza. No such thing as bad pizza, right? But this cake is," she hunted for the right word, "*majestically* vile."

"Big Tony Benedicto is a wannabe gangster. He launders money through here. I let him do that, on account of him feeding me information." Chad explored the plate of cakes, selecting one that smelled like it might not be poisonous. "I think his sister is the head chef."

"You let a gangster set up shop here?"

"I let a *wannabe* gangster set up shop here. Big Tony Benedicto is large in stature but small on follow-through." Chad frowned. He felt something stir in the air. Emotion ran fingers down his back. It felt like *yearning/yearning*, but he didn't have the Empress's knack with intuiting feelings.

Saveria mistook his expression. "That one taste bad too?"

Chad put his cake down, moving to the railing. Below, there were still gazillions of people. *Something's amiss. Is this what Nate's future-sense is like?* "You see anything odd?"

Saveria joined him, terror-cake forgotten. She scanned the crowd. "There." Her finger jabbed toward the ground. Chad followed the line of her arm, spying a group of people clotted about a man in a cassock.

A small distance away, a woman in a cassock held sermon with another huddle. Farther away, a young man barely out of his teens held his hands high, preaching to more. Everywhere Chad looked, people clustered around pastors. "The Church."

"Looks that way." Saveria's voice was sourer than when she ate the cake. "I want to know how they got here so fast."

"I want to know what they're saying." Chad squinted. The closest group was five hundred meters or so away. He couldn't see obvious weapons, just a bunch of people listening like the rapture was about to come.

The giant vid screens flickered. The smiling, benevolent face of Seth Cleaver looked down on the crowd. "People of Earth." He paused, shaking his head, expression saying he was displeased with himself. "No, that's not right. Friends. *Family*. You're a part of my flock."

"Uh oh." Saveria backed away from the railing.

Cleaver boomed on, no doubt unaware the Emperor's spymaster and his protege watched. "Earlier today the Empire stormed my place of worship. The pirate Nathan Chevell and his harlot bride Grace Gushiken turned their blades on me and mine."

The vid screens blanked. Cleaver's face was replaced by cam

footage of dropships descending on his Chapel. Cleaver spoke on. "This man tells you he wants an election, but it's a sham. We know I'm leading in the polls. There is no doubt of who would win an *honest* election." Cleaver's voice grew warm and soft, gentle and kind, all while blood, war, and fury took place on the screens. "The Empire wants me dead so their rule can continue, unopposed."

"That makes no sense," said Saveria. "If that was the case, Nate ... sorry, the *Emperor* wouldn't have mentioned an election. I don't think he wants the job."

"He doesn't, but he doesn't want the Ezeroc ruling humanity. And that motherfucker," Chad stabbed his finger at a vid screen, "is Ezeroc, haircut to boots. Besides, it doesn't have to make sense. Humans don't think these things through very well. Stir in some fear, a little conspiracy, and some well-edited cam footage and you've got yourself a media scandal."

"You know what this means, right? It means our double-date is off tonight." She pulled out her comm, already connecting to Hope, and by inference, Karkoski.

Chad left her to it, digging his own comm out. Nate answered right away. "What's up, Chad?"

"You seen Cleaver's broadcast?"

"No, Grace and I were—"

"Doing something less important," Chad cut in. "I don't want to be rude, but get your Helm, get your ass in the *Tyche*, and get off Earth. Don't ask me why, and don't stop to think about it."

A gentle hiss of static came from the comm. "Are you okay?"

Chad bowed his head. *When the danger's closest, he doesn't run. He wants to know if I'm okay.* "I'm fine. Peachy, even. But Cleaver's swirling up a mob. Minting 'em from fear and lies. He's got espers in the crowd, or just good liars. I can't tell, but I reckon this is everywhere on Earth."

"Wait one." The sound of blaster fire came from the comm. "Okay, let's say I believe you."

Chad raised an eyebrow. "What just happened?"

"Empire's Black broke in. Tried to shoot me and Grace."

"That's what I'm talking about." Chad closed his eyes. *Think.* "Get off Earth and into orbit. You'll be away from the worst of it. We can fix this, but not if you're dead."

"And what about you?"

Saveria huddled over her comm while she talked to Hope. "We'll be fine, Nate. Really. But I'd consider it a personal favor if you could get the admiral out too."

"It's already done."

"Nate..." Chad groped for the right thing to say. "Look, if you get Ellen out, this means we're square about the raise."

Nate's laugh came through the comm, bright and clear. "Where I'm going, I'll need the head of the admiralty. We'll get Hope, too. I've done a quick headcount. Kohl and Algernon aren't on the grounds."

Chad looked at Cleaver's face as it reappeared above him, a giant issuing benediction. "I'll find 'em."

"Godspeed, Chad." The comm clicked off.

The crowd below surged and seethed like a living carpet. He tapped the comm again, hoping he could make a connection. It took longer, but Algernon's voice eventually came online. "Hello, sneaky meat sock."

Chad thought about how to bring the construct up to speed. "I don't have time to explain, but—"

"Seth Cleaver is raising a mob against the Empire. He's using mass mind control, hysteria, and panic, all useful, proven tools for hacking meat sock minds."

"Uh." Chad closed his eyes for a moment. "How did you know?"

"Lucky guess. Allow me to brief you on other events. There is another coordinator-class construct. They have taken one of Kohl's friends—"

"Kohl has friends?"

"They have taken Dizzy to Mercury. This is the home of my people. I've sent out a broadcast message to my kind. I've asked them to leave Earth, but also to burn out their radios. Their minds aren't safe if someone like me would do them harm."

Chad stared at the comm for a couple heartbeats. "I have many questions."

"I don't have a lot of answers. October Kohl is hurt, but I suspect it's more pride than physical. Cams around the city show violent uprising. I fear the worst."

"Huh." Chad tapped his foot against the railing. "You ever broken out of prison before?"

BREAKING out of prison was simple. You needed to jimmy a few locks, smile at the right people, pay off the wrong, and knock out a guard or two. In Chad's view, Earth was basically the same, but done at a higher resolution.

Saveria padded at his side, a new cap pulled low. It'd been a gift from Hope and was done in surprisingly good taste despite being from an Engineer. It was black, with a wide brim. Saveria's ponytail slipped out of the back.

They hurried through the megaplex, making for an express elevator a half klick away. The elevator would take them to an underground carpark, where an autotaxi waited for them. People took little notice of them as they hurried along. *That's right. We're two more souls in a world gone mad.*

People inside the megaplex were generally oblivious to what was going on outside, shopping at stores with meager post-war stock or drinking better coffee than Big Tony Benedicto sold. Chad spied a man in a cassock marking their movements. He touched Saveria's elbow. She took in the cassock, nodded, and picked up speed.

No one waited by the elevator. Shoring up by the door, Chad palmed the controls. The panel chimed, showing the car was expected in a handful of seconds. He bounced from foot to foot. "I'm a spy. I spy on things. This is about to turn frontline."

Saveria hunched, cap dipping like a bird's beak. "We'll get in the elevator, head down some floors, and out. We'll be fine."

The elevator chimed, the doors opening with a hiss. Chad glanced up, taking in a car filled with Church-cassocked cock thistles. The moment held as Chad realized they were here for *him*, and they realized Chad was *right there*.

One at the front, a big Friar Tuck-sized asshole, roared, "Get him!"

CHAD *This only happens when I'm with you*

SAVERIA *Don't be angry at me because your timing's off*

CHAD *This is going in your performance review*

Saveria drew her sidearm, pointing it at the elevator car's ceiling. She fired, blue-white plasma *fzzzt-cracking* like a banshee's fury. Burning panels rained into the car. It gave a lurch, then dropped from view in a screech of metal.

Chad peered into the elevator shaft. Above, a severed cable's molten end glowed orange. The car waited a floor below, emergency brakes holding it from certain doom. He unholstered his own sidearm, firing into the shaft. He placed his shots carefully, aiming for the visible anchors. Plasma lit the shaft like a strobe. Six shots did the trick.

Metal groaned as the car dropped away, gathering speed as it went. Chad turned back to Saveria, just in time to see a Church-woman tackle her. Both fell into the shaft. Chad would have followed, but he had his own problems. A stocky man wearing a terrible mustard-colored shirt rushed him, brandishing a short piece of metal that might once have been the handle of a mop. *No Church cassock, but maybe he's on a break.*

Chad drew his sword with a hiss of steel, blocking the man's panicked swing. His rapier chimed, the hilt shivering in his hand. The man swung again like he was possessed by demons. The rapier needled his torso, red spots blooming through the terrible yellow dawn of his shirt. It didn't slow the stocky guy at all. Face twisted in rage, he swung, the mop handle trying to find an opening. Chad backed up until his heel found the edge of the shaft. Air whistled at his rear.

Fuck all this. Chad flourished his steel, disarmed the man in a flash of metal, then kicked him in the groin as the mop handle *clanged* to the tiled floor. The man curled around his pain. Chad helped him on by slugging him across the jaw with his rapier's finger guard, dropping him to an ugly yellow and red pile.

"That's a tragic shirt to die in." Saveria appeared as if conjured from air. Her cap was missing but she was otherwise intact.

"That's what I thought." Chad looked from her to the shaft, then back to her. "You good?"

"I'm good. Landed on a strut and jumped back up here. Don't know what happened to my attacker." She straightened her jacket.

"This guy," Chad nudged the body at his feet, "isn't wearing Church colors."

"Maybe he's on a break."

"Snap! That's what I thought at first, but... I think he's under remote control." Chad turned the body over, checking the wrists. "No anti-esper bracelet."

"He made a lot of bad choices this morning, then." Saveria scanned the crowd forming in front of them. "We should get moving."

"We can't go down." Chad eyed the ceiling. "I don't like the idea of the roof. No way out."

"We could call Kohl and Algernon."

"No." Chad shook his head. "*We're* rescuing *them*. If *they* rescue *us*, Kohl will never let us live it down."

"Let *you* live it down, you mean. I'm still in training. I never did get that field promotion." Saveria shrugged. "The other option is we cut our way out of here, killing hundreds of innocents. I'm done with that." She looked away.

Chad nodded. "Me too. Let's get Algernon back on the line while we get to higher ground. Moving might prevent us being brutally murdered quite so soon."

"This isn't much of a prison break."

"Wrong. This is an *epic* prison break. C'mon." Chad shared a smile with her. He'd never been one for trust back in the day. Kazuo kept them at each other's throats. Turns out all he needed was a person as damaged as him. Half human, half machine, Saveria was the partner in crime he didn't know he needed. "How about we do some spying for a change?"

THREE

Nate keyed his comm. "El? I need you."

Her sleep-or-was-it-the-alcohol-fuzzed voice came back in mere seconds. "You're married, and I'm not drunk enough for a booty call." *Alcohol it is, then.*

Grace raised an eyebrow along with a quirk of her lips. She held position by the door, naked steel glinting in the gloom. They'd elected to leave the lights off while dressing for a rapid evac of the palace grounds. *No sense in drawing attention.* She called, "Are you too drunk to fly?"

"Is this some weird threesome thing?" El paused. "Hang on. Grace said 'fly' and you're calling me in the middle of the night."

"It's ten. Our bedtimes come earlier as we age," Nate said. "Here's what's going on. The palace is overrun by insurgents. It feels like everyone's trying to kill us, excepting those who aren't, but they're all wearing the same team colors. We're getting Karkoski, Hope, and then leaving. We need you."

"If I couldn't fly, would you just leave me here to die?"

"Quite likely," Nate said. "You sobering up yet?"

"It'd take more alcohol than exists on this rock to make me too drunk to fly. See you in ten." The comm clicked off.

Nate strode toward Grace. His black blade hung in a scabbard on his hip, a sidearm holstered on the other side. He wore an armor jacket more out of habit than need. Grace donned an all-black ensemble, the only visible skin her face. He was amazed she'd chosen him and winced every time he figured that choice might get her dead. *Quit your whining. She'd take Cleaver without breaking a sweat.* "You ready?"

"You're nervous." She touched his cheek with a gloved hand. "Don't be. We've got this."

"We have to get out of here without killing any of the mind-controlled thralls of Seth Cleaver. It's tricky to not harm people when they're intent on your murder."

"Which is why we're leaving. Your plan is to get us away, so Cleaver can't hurt more people. We find him, then clean his clock."

"It sounded easier when I said it," Nate admitted. "It's possible some folks turned simply because they don't like me."

"That's because you can be the most annoying man in the universe. You do unexpected things, like trying to keep the followers of your enemy alive." Grace opened the door a crack. Light crept in, shadowed by the smell of burning plastic. "Let's go."

He followed her into the well-lit corridor. The palace was huge, its hallways built at massive scale. There were supposed to be guards most everywhere, but not a soul stood outside. Grace led on, prowling like a hunting cat. The light seemed to wash off her, the black material flowing like a second skin. *Hell, she manages to make skulking look legendary.* Nate hurried after, doing his level best to not clank, rattle, or creak.

The sound of blaster fire came to him, but faint. A scream, caught short. He didn't know who died, but he was certain they'd given their life for the wrong reasons. *No one deserves to fall so another can sit on a fancy chair.*

They reached an antechamber. Nate wasn't clear on its particular purpose. It held five doorways, one of which they'd entered through. Next to a short bench sat a table with a flower arrangement, perhaps waiting for a weary civil servant to abide a spell.

A blood-curdling yell came from a doorway. Nate spun, taking in a man coming around a corner. He ran like the devil was after him. Behind him, a man in a cassock rounded the corner, leveling a plasma rifle. Blue-white fire tore the runner apart in a shower of burning body parts.

Nate, never one to make himself an easy target, hustled to the side. He took cover against the wall. Grace hunkered opposite him, eyes hard, waiting. Nate drew his sidearm.

Step out two strides.

Raise your weapon.

Fire, then take one more step.

He rose, walking around the corner. Two paces took him off center, blue-white fire slashing the air where he'd been. He aimed his sidearm, the weapon flashing an angry response. The Churchgoer's body exploded into flame, rifle falling to the floor. Nate took another step, his enemy's weapon discharging into the space where he'd stood.

"I will never understand how you do that." Grace swept past him, jogging around the burning remains of the runner and their enemy both.

"I can see the future. I've told you before." Nate shrugged, holstering his sidearm. "Not my fault you can't do it."

"I can do it!" She shook her head. "I just can't do it that well."

"You can create shields with your mind. You've held a starship from falling into a gravity well. Saveria taught you her latest trick of using your mind like a razor, or bulldozer, cutting body parts without the need for steel." Nate followed, trying not to look at the burning remains on the floor. "You can send yourself better than anyone, and make shadow clones. You can read minds, intuit emotions, and for all I know speak the language of beasts. Can't you let me have this one damn thing?"

"It irks me because I'll never win at cards against you." She paused, hand raised as she peeked around a corner. "No one here."

"You'd never win at cards anyway." He strode past her, trying for a little swagger. For all his future-sense kept him alive, it was terrible for long-range planning. It supplied vague, not-very-useful hints, more feelings than anything. "Let's get to Hope."

Hope was guesting with them. She'd been going out on an experimental date with Saveria, Chad, and Karkoski. It kept her away from the Guild Hall tonight, and Nate counted that a blessing.

It's not enough to run. You've got to run the right way.

Nate froze. That time, future-sense felt *different*. A warning, at scale. Grace padded on a few more steps, then turned to him.

GRACE *Did you feel that?*

NATE *Something's coming*

He broke into a run. No time for finesse, not a moment for swagger. Pure adrenalin, metal leg boosting him along better than his flesh and blood one. He rounded a corner, coming face to face with a woman in an Emperor's Black uniform. Her face was twisted into a snarl, her carbine rising toward him. Nate didn't slow, cannoning through her, gold fist doing all the talking that was needed. She fell, two of her teeth clattering free on the marble floor.

A door ahead opened, a palace servant charging through with a metal tray raised high. Grace danced up the wall, dodging the wild swing, tray catching nothing but the light. She came down with a dragon punch, knocking the hapless man to stretch his full length along the ground.

The door to Hope's room lay ahead. It hung broken, charred fragments of wood still smoking. Nate entered at a run, sword clearing its scabbard. *Someone's fixing to harm your Hope.* Entering her room revealed the bed, rumbled but empty of humans, blaster burns through the sheets. On the floor, Karkoski in fine dress clothes and a jacket wrestled a man in a cassock. Hope backed away from a woman with a knife in each hand. She didn't have her rig; she was clothed in white, perhaps a new fashion from Venus, underneath a clear plastic jacket. The lights flickered above all, a crazed rhythm faster than the beat of Nate's heart.

The black blade hungered free. Nate's golden fingers held the hilt, tossing it to spin a deadly cartwheel. It caught the woman with the knives in the side, the force of the throw tearing her from the ground and slamming her into the wall. The blade pinned her body there, hilt thrumming.

Grace jumped a low divan as Karkoski kicked the man atop her clear. He came up, drawing a blaster. The weapon's muzzle hunted for a target, swinging to Hope.

Nate's sidearm cleared his holster, but Grace was faster. She flung her arm out, screaming, "No!"

The man was torn apart by the force of her will. Red mist sprayed the far wall, blaster battery exploding in a shower of blue-white sparks. The wall behind the man crumpled, stone and cerami-crete bulging as if a god's fist slammed it.

Silence. Hope's wide eyes. Karkoski's grimace. Grace's teeth, bared like a lioness. Nate's black blade, blood slicking down the thirsty steel to trickle off the hilt.

"Jesus H. Christ," said Karkoski. "You sure you hit him hard enough?" She rose, wincing and favoring her left side.

"No," admitted Grace. "I wasn't quite sure how that would work at range. Saveria and I are..." She shook her head. "She is master and student both."

"Uh huh." Karkoski went to Hope. "You good?"

"Um." Hope's eyes were still wide.

Nate went to his sword, curling golden fingers about the hilt. A tug, and it came free, body sliding to the floor. He turned to the door, anger curling inside him like bottled smoke. "I feel like we need an accounting."

"Cleaver's throat's too far away to choke," said Karkoski. "I've got a starship in orbit. Let's go."

Nate nodded. "Hope?"

"Um. What's going on?"

"Mutiny. Insurrection. Devils and angels, warring above. A thin line stands between humanity and our extinction. Gods coming home, and the righteous burning false idols." Nate closed his eyes. "They're not our gods, though. We'll bring our own." When he opened his eyes, he found everyone staring at him. "Something I said?"

"What he means," Grace walked to the door, checking outside, "is Seth Cleaver's corrupting the minds of citizens, either with esper powers or good ol' fashioned fear."

"Okay. We should go." Hope hustled to a cupboard, stepping gingerly around a pool of blood as she did so. From inside the cupboard she retrieved a small rectangle. Turning it on, it articulated out insect-like legs, clambering up her body and folding out into her rig. The visor lapped into place. "I'm good to go, Cap."

"Then we fly." He turned on his heel, making the corridor. Nate set a brisk pace, because if insurgents were in the inner sanctum, the Black were lost, the guard fallen, and all bets were off. They passed bodies aplenty. There was no telling on whose side they fought unless one wore a Church cassock.

They made it as far as the grand ballroom before anyone else did something dickish. Entering the huge doors, Nate found a group of people inside. There was a huddle of folk on the ground, perhaps twenty souls, and a larger group of more than forty standing guard.

The guards held blasters of various types. The captives held bruises and broken limbs. One was missing an arm, the charred stump showing the *how* if not the *why* of it.

A young man on the floor spied them. Hope bloomed on his face, and he made to rise. A captor, unsure how the winds changed but unhappy with their new course, gunned him down in a fusillade of hot blue-white fire.

"Hold!" Nate stalked forward. All eyes turned on him. He heard a small *um* from Hope behind him, but payed it no mind. "Seems folk are bent on hurting each other, either in my name or someone else's. There's no call for that. Put down your arms. Election's not far away."

"Die, Empire scum!" screamed a woman holding a carbine. She swung her blaster toward Nate before her torso exploded into roiling fire. Surprised, Nate glanced down at his golden hand, holding his blaster like it'd been there all the time.

"You're outnumbered, Chevell." A cassocked man with three-day stubble sneered. "It's time for you and all your kind to burn in the holy fires of retribution."

"A small point of order." Nate put a smile on, though his heart wasn't in it. "It's *Emperor* Chevell."

"I don't bow to the likes of you."

"You don't look like you wash, either, so let's agree your judgment's not great." Nate put a little swagger into his stride, drawing closer. "You've got forty seconds to lay down arms."

"Take us less time than that to kill you." Three-day-stubble glanced around for support, found it in the menacing eyes of his comrades, and took a step forward. "Why don't we end it here?"

Nate held up a hand. "One moment." He checked the time on his personal comm, nodded, and pocketed the device. "You want to gun me down?"

"I want to kill—"

"A simple yes or no." Nate nodded, encouraging.

"Uh. I mean, yes."

"Great." Nate strolled toward the group of prisoners. "Why not kill us all?"

"Wait, what?" A woman on the floor looked panicked, like this wasn't what she expected from her Emperor.

"I mean, put all the people who love the Empire on this side," Nate walked toward the wall, arms wide, "and the rest of you over there."

"I was wrong about you." Three-day-stubble gave a grudging nod. "I thought you were a coward, but I'll give you your hero's funeral. You've earned it."

Grace joined Nate. "You know I trust you with my life, right? Except, I'd like to know the plan."

He turned his smile up into the megawatt range. "The plan is, all Team Empire's with me." He unsheathed his blade, laying it on the cold marble, then tossed his blaster after. "The rest will burn in hell."

Grace looked at his sword, blaster, then back to him. "You *do* have a plan, right?"

NATE *Trust me*

GRACE *No one in the history of ever has increased trust on hearing those two words*

Despite that, she tossed her steel beside his. Karkoski joined them, looking like this had *better* be the best fucking joke or someone was gonna pay. Hope trailed after, visor not hiding her confusion. In ones and twos, people got from the floor to join Nate by the wall.

He let them walk behind him. Standing at the front of the group of prisoners, they faced their forty-something-strong firing squad. Nate straightened his jacket, meeting Three-day-stubble's eyes. "Last chance."

"We'll pray for you." The man shouldered his plasma rifle. Like a wave, his comrades did too.

Nate retrieved his personal comm from his pocket. "Wait!" He checked the time. "Sorry. We're good. After you."

Three-day-stubble glanced to the woman at his right, shrugged, then said, "On three."

Behind Nate, an older man said, "I've lived a long time, sire. I admit I don't yet feel ready to die, but I won't kneel for them."

"Two!"

A woman crept up to Grace's side. "Empress." Her eyes found the floor. "Thank you for not letting us die alone."

"One!"

The windows behind the firing squad ruptured inward. Glass blew inside in a thousand shards of deadly hail. Nate squinted, golden hand up in front of his face. Shards rained on their location, tinkling against the faint shimmer of Grace's mind-shield.

The roar of the *Tyche* filled the ballroom, the starship thunderous outside. Massive, brilliant lamps used to push back the hard black shone like suns. Air swirled, pulling at Grace's hair. Nate spied El through the flight deck windows. She spared him a glance and a quick one-handed salute, her own golden hand catching the light and tossing it back.

Three-day-stubble roared, swinging his rifle toward the starship. He vanished into red mist as the scream of PDCs shook the room. Tungsten rained, fragments of marble, tables, and chairs swirled like flotsam.

Nate covered his ears. The *Tyche's* rage at those that threatened her crew made him feel small, tiny, an insignificant mortal at the feet of a goddess. It lasted only seconds, then the PDCs settled to stillness with a whine and a clank.

The starship settled her skids on the ballroom floor, sinking through the marble and into the ceramicrete beneath with a crunch. El's voice, booming like the goddess herself, came through the ship's external PA. "You folks need a ride?"

"Aye, Helm." Nate poked a finger in his ear. *No sense wondering if your hearing's damaged. You're alive, by the grace of a goddess.*

"*That* was your plan?" Karkoski rounded on him. "What if El was late? What if she couldn't find you?"

"Admiral." Nate jerked his head toward Team Empire, who were running the full range of emotions from *surprise* to *elation*. He walked to his ship, reaching a hand up to touch her flank. "The *Tyche's* my ship. She'll come across the hard black for me and mine. Her Helm's the best there is or has ever been." He offered her a smile. "This is what I do."

"You do *lucky*?" Karkoski's voice rose an octave.

"Pretty much." Grace sidled past her. "You coming? We've got a universe to save." Hope jogged in her wake.

"I will to the day I die wonder what I created, putting you on the throne." Karkoski walked toward the *Tyche's* waiting cargo bay ramp. She paused, glancing back at Nate, then the people behind him. "I *think* I did the right thing."

"Don't break out the champagne yet." Nate broke into a brisk stride. "We need to get in the air. There's a storm coming."

——————

THE ACCELERATION COUCH'S straps held Nate like an old friend. A slightly uncomfortable, clingy, yet strong old friend. Nate sat in the co-pilot's chair, El across from him. Hope was in Engineering, while Grace and Karkoski traded looks in the ready room. *I wish I'd never left this. I was supposed to captain a small ship in the hard black.*

San Francisco lay beneath them. He wished he could say it sparkled like the night sky above, but there weren't enough lights back in the city to do that, and the ash in the atmosphere clouded things some.

The ship grumbled up on Endless fields. El tapped her console with golden fingers, her flesh and blood hand on the yoke. "Where to?"

Nate jabbed a finger out across the bay. "That way. Not up. There are two reason for that. Above us, starships are gunning for each other."

"Sounds bad," El agreed, bringing the *Tyche's* nose to bear on the water. It lay flat, dark like obsidian. "What's your other boggle?"

"They're launching nukes at us." Nate shrugged. "Or, they will soon. We need to take ourselves out there, so when they miss us, on account of you being the best Helm that ever flew, those weapons hit water instead of people."

"How do you know that?" El nudged the throttle. The *Tyche's* drives rose to a savage growl.

Thrust pressed Nate onto his chair. "I can see the future." He held up his hand. "Grace felt it too."

"Your whole deal was to get me out of a perfectly good bar so I could be a *target*?"

"My whole deal was to get you into orbit, because we're going after Seth Cleaver." Nate wheezed as thrust passed 4Gs, the ship trembling as they punched atmosphere aside.

"We need to talk about *not* rushing toward evil overlords who corrupt the minds of all humans everywhere." She scratched metal fingers under her anti-Ezeroc bracelet. "How's he getting through? Most everyone's got one of these."

"I've a theory or two. My best guess is, he's broken them somehow." Nate tapped his own console, pulling up the comm. "Algernon?"

"Hello, Captain."

"Situation?"

"Everything is dire."

"Good talk. How hard would it be to make nanites that attack the anti-esper bracelets, rendering them useless?"

"Difficult. I provided the admiralty a briefing on this possibility. You would need a sufficiently advanced crystal mind to complete the programming of the nanites..." He trailed off.

Nate tapped the console. "Hello?"

"Hello, Captain. There's been an important development! It's quite exciting. When I briefed the admiralty, I suggested the odds of subverting the bracelets was low."

"Because all the crystal minds are on our side."

"They *were* on our side."

"Hah," Nate said.

"Hah," Algernon agreed. "Earlier this evening we encountered another such intelligence. One like me. The good news is, without the ciphers, it will still be difficult."

"Ciphers?" Nate glimpsed the contrail of a missile above. "I'll call you back." He dropped the comm, trying to avoid El's glare. After a moment, he sighed. "Out with it."

"There's another one? The last rogue AI cut off my arm!"

"Technically, she cut off your shoulder *and* your arm." Nate winced right after the words escaped.

He felt El's fury seething to a fury-level boiling point. "I think we need to—"

"Fly the ship," suggested Nate. "Up there. Looks like a weapon headed in our direction."

"Don't change the subject!" El took a breath, but whatever she was about to say was interrupted by the flight deck holo clearing, smooth water replaced by an angry red telemetry map. *BRACE BRACE BRACE INBOUND MISSILE BRACE BRACE BRACE.* "Goddammit!"

She rammed the throttle forward. Nate slammed back onto his chair. His breath rasped out as the ship paced over the Atlantic. El brought the *Tyche* up aways where the air was thinner. Smoother, so the *Tyche* could race like she was born to.

"It's. Coming. Around," he rasped.

Her fury-laden screech was flattened by thrust. "Don't. Tell. Me. How. To. Fly!"

The *Tyche's* holo kept Nate abreast of their situation. They passed into hypersonic speed, MACH 7 slipping by like a twig dropped in a stream. MACH 8, then MACH 9, the ship shuddering with thrust.

They went higher, the missile still on their tail. It looped about, not hitting the ground or water, which was a blessing, but still chasing them, which wasn't great.

"Hello, sire. This is Mercenary actual." Captain McDonald's voice came from the comm. "It looks like you're in some trouble. Again. Would you like assistance?"

Nate toggled the comm. "Yes."

"Excellent. Try not to move about too much. We're in a space war ourselves, sire, and our Tactician is new at this." The comm clicked off.

El knew the drill. She pointed the ship at the stars. They climbed from Earth's gravity well, trailing twin pillars of fire. Atmosphere thinned, thrust growing stronger. The bright lance of a particle cannon's beam slipped off their port bow, tearing the nuke on their heels from the sky.

BRACE   BRACE   BRACE   NUCLEAR   DETONATION DETECTED BRACE BRACE BRACE.

The shockwave hit them, carrying them further into the heavens on wings of the devil's fury. The *Tyche* bucked like a bronco. Metal groaned behind them, then eased to silence.

El reduced thrust, presumably so they wouldn't stroke out. "Where to, Cap?" She sounded tired, but also soberer than before. "You want to resupply at the *Mercenary?*"

The *Mercenary* lay out there, too distant to make out with human eyes, but the *Tyche* saw her. The ship also caught the conflict about her, Navy dreadnoughts firing on each other. *Civil war, at the gates of Eden.*

"No." He felt tired too, worn thin by conflict. "Slip us out of here, quiet as you can. Turn around Mercury and wait."

"What's near Mercury?"

"Friends, maybe." Nate rubbed his neck. "Tell the *Mercenary* to fall back. We won't turn our weapons on each other. Those who stand with the Empire, retreat to Mercury."

"You sure the machines are our allies?" El plotted the course anyway.

"Not sure of much at the moment, except I don't want people dying on my account. The constructs can't be corrupted by espers."

"Aye, Cap. Mercury it is."

The *Tyche* scuttled around the perfect blue haze of Earth's atmosphere. Nate watched their planet slip away. *You're not running. Your finding aid.*

It didn't help. He might never see humanity's home again.

FOUR

Burn out your radios. Don't trust anyone who looks like me.

That's the last message Algernon sent to his people. He didn't like the idea of service-class constructs without their shepherd, but they'd gathered so much humanity into their cores they didn't need him anymore. He hoped they felt strong enough to walk alone now. They'd been designed to walk with at least one coordinator, and he was depriving them of that last, final link to who they used to be.

He watched a trail of fire streak toward the heavens. *Another starship taking my people away from Earth.* Algernon lowered his eyes. He and October stood in an alley, much like the rest. Old stone walls rubbing shoulders with newer ceramicrete. Smoke and ash, much of it recent, settled around them. It refused to cling to Algernon's gleaming form, but October Kohl looked like a swamp monster.

They walked to find cleaner air. The construct didn't need it, but the human would suffer without it. "October." The big man grunted a response that might have been *gofuckyourself.* "We need help."

"We," October coughed, hawked, spat something viscous, and wiped his mouth with the back of his hand, "need to find a bar."

"I know what Cleaver's after."

October squinted. "He's after Dizzy."

Algernon spread his hands, watching as flakes of soot hit his metal to slide off again. *They made me well. Hundreds of years this skin's repelled the dirt of multiple worlds. But have I become dirty on the inside? Should I side with humans or my own kind? What is 'right?'* "Dizzy knows a thing that only one other knows."

October rubbed his wrist where the anti-esper bracelet lay against his skin. Algernon's sensitive eyes saw the heat of the metal. It was running a toasty 50C, more than enough to be uncomfortable. "This fucken thing. I should take it off."

"There appear to be espers at work. It would be unwise to open your mind to them."

"Yeah?" The big man rounded on him. "You 'opened your mind' to your golden friend?"

"It's a fair question. You're concerned about my loyalties." Algernon waited for Kohl's grudging nod. "You should be."

"What?"

"I'm a machine." The construct touched his chest. "I'm made of starlight and moonbeams, not the crude material that barely keeps you upright." Algernon looked to the sky, another starship's pillar of fire glimmering in the ash cloud above. "For all that, you are *my* people. Your Emperor showed me what humans are like."

"You're not killing me because Nate's a sucker for a hard luck case?"

"I'm not killing you because," Algernon placed a hand on October's shoulder, "you are my best friend in the entire universe. I don't care what you're made of." He let his hand fall. "I understand if that's insufficient. They are just words. I have no face to read."

"It's fine." October sagged against a wall, worrying at his bracelet again.

Algernon nodded. "There is a nanobot plague ravaging Earth. When my people dropped it on Osaka hundreds of years ago, we made sure you couldn't unlock it."

"With you so far. Osaka's a shit hole, anyway."

"It was very nice, once." Algernon looked away. "We hid the inner workings of the nanobot plague behind an advanced cipher. There are two locations in the universe where the cipher is held. I know where they are. I believe your friend Dizzy has the location of one."

A man rounded the corner of the alley ahead, eyes wild. His clothes were rags, blood running from cuts on his face. He saw them, screamed, and ran forward. October raised his carbine. Red light glimmered trails in the rain of ash. With a *whine-chunk*, the wild-eyed man exploded in a shower of viscera. "But there's two?"

Algernon tapped his head. "I kept a copy for safekeeping. It's how Hope Baedeker and I were able to reprogram the nanites to kill Ezeroc."

"So, Dizzy knows about the other one. Where is it?"

"It was on Venus. The cipher was in a carbon crystal lattice cube one centimeter a side. It was outside the domes, because humans go there rarely. I destroyed it."

October nodded. "So, these assholes have Dizzy. He tries to sell the location of the cipher, because while he's wily like a fox, he's also as dumb as a box of rocks. And he doesn't know it's proper fucked. Your buddy—"

"He is no buddy of mine."

"Your buddy hears of this, comes on down here, and what, tries to buy it?"

Algernon nodded. "I believe that the most likely scenario. After killing everyone else who was a contender to the purchase, it's likely Dizzy got cold feet. Refused to sell, believing he'd be next."

"How'd Dizzy find this thing on Venus?"

"I laid a trail," Algernon explained. "The vault where the cipher was is still there. It is now mined with a significant volume of explosives. A honey badger."

"A honeypot."

"That, also." Algernon crouched, draping one of October's arms across his shoulders. They weren't too hot to touch anymore, and his friend needed him. "Those who found the trail were likely untrustworthy scoundrels."

"Sounds like Dizzy."

"I suspect Dizzy refused to part with the knowledge willingly. It's possible my ... counterpart applied percussive persuasion, and when that failed, gathered his prize and absconded off-world."

"What's off-world?"

"Seth Cleaver, a powerful esper, and thus a reader of minds. Extracting the location of the cipher from Dizzy will be trivial for one of his talents, and after that your friend will be worthless garbage."

"Some might say he's worthless garbage already." October took his arm away from Algernon's shoulders, standing on his own. A little iron crept back into his spine. "Let's go take out the trash."

"I don't think you're mixing metaphors in the correct manner." Algernon held up a hand to forestall October's objections. "But I understand your intent."

"I've got a plan."

"Oh, no."

"It's a good plan," October insisted. "Chad wanted us to help break him out of prison, right?"

"If by 'prison' you mean 'rescue from the mob besieging his position atop a megaplex,' then yes." Algernon waited, curious. It wasn't often October Kohl had the mental drop on him, and he couldn't wait to see what came next.

"The best way to bust out of jail is with criminals." Kohl spat another glob of vileness to the ceramicrete pavement. "Let's go get some evil people."

ALGERNON WANTED TO HELP OCTOBER, but he also knew this particular horse wasn't thirsty enough yet. The big man lumbered on, face in the crook of his elbow most of the time, trying to suck as little ash as possible. Sometimes October shot people who ran at them. Other times, he ducked aside. Algernon hadn't worked out what made people *targets* versus *refugees*.

Human faces were full of expression. Not just the parts humans saw, but deeper. Blood flow under their skin showed remarkable changes with anger, fear, and love. Algernon saw all this in the people they encountered, but with one universal constant. *All these people are desperate.*

October hissed, shaking his wrist. "Fucken thing burns, Al."

"Your bracelet?"

"It's like a brand of fire." Kohl hollered, then yanked. The ring of metal clattered to the ceramicrete.

Algernon noted the bracelet's temperature above 60C. "Don't worry. Your pain receptors are likely overloaded and numb at this point."

October rounded on him, shoving a hand onto Algernon's chest. Algernon noted the ring of red skin where the bracelet had been. "*Al!* Get—"

In the time it took October to get those two words out, Algernon saw him raise his carbine, glacially slow at the standard human operational cycle. *Oh dear. An esper has found their way in. I must stop him from hurting himself.* Algernon socked him across the jaw. He was very careful, making the strike fast enough to slosh October's brain about and induce unconsciousness, but not so hard it would break the big man's jaw. As his eyes glazed, staring into some middle fantasy land only he could see, Algernon grabbed him before he could fall, laying him on the ground. "I'm very sorry. The bracelet kept your mind safe, but now you are problematic."

The blue-white of plasma snapped through the air where Algernon stood seconds prior, tearing a hole in the brick wall. Algernon grabbed October's carbine, spinning from his crouched position. In the ash fog, a man braced himself as he aimed for the metal man.

Algernon didn't wait for the laser carbine's targeting computer to catch on. He squeezed the trigger, red light sprinkling across the intervening distance as it danced through ash particulate. He used the laser to shear their attacker in half down the middle. *Skull to balls*, October might have said, if Algernon hadn't just knocked him out. *You misunderstood his intent.*

Still! Critical threat removed. Algernon stood, then glanced at October's prone form. *Well, unless I count myself. My kind doesn't make mistakes... so what is this?* He bent, hefting October's form as if the big man were a sack of tissue paper, then slung him over a golden shoulder.

Before their ... misunderstanding, they'd been en route to the air car. October thought the men guarding the vehicle might still be about. Algernon thought this unlikely, but agreed it was their best option in a scenario full of poor options. He made better time now he could carry his unconscious friend but kept his speed below his maximum. If he worked too hard, his internal components would heat up, which would trigger his air-cooling system, which in turn would suck vile ash into his interior. It wouldn't kill him, but...

I don't want my insides to be full of carbon ash that used to be people. They deserve so much better.

The broken-down building lay ahead. When they'd last come this way, fires burned in barrels, and street merchants sold food of questionable providence alongside others selling their bodies. Now, all were gone. The barrels no longer burned, but the sky wept smoke.

Lights glimmered in the ruin that used to be a building. It wasn't the light of the air car. These were smaller, personal lamps. *Perhaps these meat socks carry flashlights.*

Algernon slowed his pace, stepping with care. His optics mapped the ground, and he placed his feet so as not to disturb rock. A stray sound could give him away, and with October over his shoulder, inbound rounds posed too high a risk. He briefly considered leaving his passenger and heading on alone, but there were too many ferocious people on the prowl.

Rounding a pillar of stone, he saw four men standing in the gloom. All held individual illumination sources — two using the beams on personal consoles, the others using flashlights. They stood around the air car, four gray ghosts guarding a prize.

These are the same men that were here before. "Hello, meat socks!"

All four spun. Two held steel bars like bats. The one October clotheslined earlier readied a knife. The last hefted a chunk of ceramicrete. Clothesline stepped forward, jerking his chin toward Algernon's load. "He okay?"

"He ... fell. I expect he'll wake with a headache and a thirst for revenge." Algernon bent, settling October to the ground. "Why are you still here?"

"He promised payment. More good Empire coin, just like the last." Clothesline walked closer, knife held low. Algernon wondered if he meant to attack them, stealing October's coins and making for freedom. "Isn't that right?"

"You are correct, sir." Algernon nodded.

"Deal still hold?"

Crossing his arms, Algernon examined the four again. Tried to see in them what October did. *Four men, desperate and empty. Fighting for crumbs, scattered at the base of their home.* He turned bright-white eyes to the sky. *So alone among the stars, until they weren't.* "Why did October spare you?"

"Say what?"

"Why," Algernon nudged the big man's prone form, eliciting a groan, "didn't he kill you? You attacked him. Tried to take what was his. I'm trying to understand, because it seems people are beyond me. Also, why haven't you attacked us? Most humans have been driven mad."

"You talking about the music?" Clothesline tapped his head with the point of his knife, the motion erratic, even a little desperate. "It's like a song you know but can't remember the words to."

"Ah. That's a trick they learned from you. When humans brought warships to my world, they gave us a beautiful yet unsolvable mathematics problem. It sucked our foolish crystal minds into an endless cycle of repetition."

"Thing is, I can't eat music." Clothesline jerked his arm toward his friends. "We can't feed our families on songs." He reached into a pocket, pulling out a shiny bright Empire coin. The ash hadn't got its grimy fingers on it yet. "This is stronger than the music."

"Money? Is that all it takes?" Algernon glanced at October again. *He doesn't value money like that. He gives it away. What's he buying?*

"No." The guy with the hunk of ceramicrete dropped it. It hit the ground with a crunch. He walked closer. "Empire coins feed our families. Keep us warm at night. All of that. But they also said that someone," he nodded at October, "*noticed*. Saw *what* we were, *where* we were, and *why*. Do you see?"

The ground trembled, another spacecraft climbing to the heavens. Algernon watched it for a moment, then turned back. Noted the man's empty hands, and the patches where soot was scraped free by the ceramicrete hunk. His optics picked out calluses, scars, and cuts. Those hands held the cares of the world. "I'm not sure I do."

Rock Guy pointed at the spacecraft climbing up Earth's gravity well. "That one of yours?"

Algernon nodded. "My kind aren't welcome here anymore."

"Neither are we, but we ain't running, metal man. It's our fucking *home.*"

"It's not like that." Algernon spread his hands. "Humans hunt us—"

"Humans hunt humans, too." He spat. "Big game season."

Algernon thought about that for a long time. Thirty-eight picoseconds passed while he processed. "If you had whatever you needed, what would you do?"

"Knock those roaches off our world." Clothesline spoke without hesitation.

"These things can be difficult." Algernon sighed. He wondered what they saw. A man of gold, with bright-white eyes. "Sometimes

you need to go out there," he pointed at the stars, "to make a difference down here."

"Climb into the lap of the gods? Suck on Hera's tit?" Clothesline
barked a laugh, then looked to October. "He knew better."

"Let me tell you a story." Algernon rifled through October's belt
pouch. He found fistfuls of good Empire coin. He stood, tossing them
to the ground. "Here. You can stay and listen, or go. Either way, the
coin is yours. You held your bargain."

They froze, eyes on the glittering metal. Ash drifted low, burying
it mote by mote. "What kind of story?" This from a previously-silent
man, his length of steel now laid over his shoulder.

"Centuries ago, my people did a terrible thing. It didn't matter
who started the war between humanity and its creations. We aimed
to end it. We made a plague, the likes of which hasn't been seen in all
human history." Algernon spread his silver hand, putting fingers
against his golden chest. "My people made to end yours. You were so
very angry. You drove us away then. Many of us remember. It's why
we're leaving now." He nudged a coin with his foot. "You came to our
world. It was a planet you'd given us, perfect for our people. You
rained death on us, but worse, you tricked some of us," he tapped
silvered fingers against his chest again, "into helping you do it."

They were uneasy, but none stepped away. *And none of them are
taking the coins. Interesting.* "What you don't know is that some of us
survived. Buried beneath Mercury's crust, a few idled the centuries
away. For that to happen, a group of humans decided something. I
don't know who they were, or where they went. Yet I love them
dearly. Those people decided to leave us be. They turned their starships away. Made reports to their superiors the war was won, and
constructs were dead and gone. They left us to our graveyard, and our
eternal sleep. Five hundred years passed. Evil men used us again,
building more service-class constructs to kill you. The cycle might
have repeated, except for one human."

"The Emperor," whispered Clothesline.

"Nathan Chevell," Algernon corrected, but gently. "Another

human decided to spare us, even when all was lost. Do you know what that means?" Clothesline shook his head. Rock Guy looked down. The other two stayed still as stones. "We will never turn on him or those who sail under his flag. We're leaving Earth, but we're not abandoning our friends. We're going to the stars to fight the war you cannot win. We don't have minds the insects can control. We will be your thin silver line against the terrible dawn."

Algernon bent, lifting October. His friend was still out. He trudged toward the air car, sending a remote command to open the door. Gull wings opened wide, and he slipped October inside. Turning, he was somewhat surprised to see all four men remained, with the coins still at their feet. He feared they'd been taken over by the enemy. *Will I have to kill these fragile, desperate men?* "Hello?"

Clothesline coughed, the sound ragged. More than ash, the man had a sickness in his lungs. "How many of you are left?"

Algernon closed the gull wing door, shutting October inside. "Four hundred and ninety-seven."

"Five hundred against the insects?" Clothesline laughed. "You're mad."

"Some think so." Algernon stepped past Clothesline. The man didn't shy away, but he didn't look happy either. "We'll be on our way. We have friends to rescue and a war to win."

"What kind of friends?"

"Does it matter? We're all people."

Clothesline gave a short, angry shake of his head. "Didn't mean it that way. I meant, army friends, or civilian friends?"

"Oh." Algernon looked down. *You always judge them at their worst.* "One is a spy, and the other has a half-crystal mind. The crystal part was my eternal bliss until she died and become someone else's."

"Someone got your girl?"

"Or, I gave them 'my girl' to make up for my terrible crimes." Algernon sagged a little. "Living is very difficult."

"You robots are weird. Okay." Clothesline nodded, like he was working himself up to something. "Here's what'll happen. We're getting in the air car. Then we'll get your friends." He made no move toward the coin behind him, the glints dying as ash piled high.

"Why?" Algernon glanced to where the Empire coin lay. "You have your money."

"My home was over there." Clothesline nodded toward where Algernon came from. Where the terrible, monstrous launch of a spacecraft rendered many humans to ash. "It's not anymore."

"Mine neither." Rock Guy walked to the air car, palming the door open. "Besides, we don't let other people do our fighting." He slipped into the air car.

The rest joined him, leaving Algernon to eye the empty ruins, and the sad final glint of Empire coin fading under stray carbon drifts. *Is this what October bought with his coin?* He shook his head. *I don't understand these frail, beautiful creatures at all.*

FIVE

Nate shook like a man with a chill. Coming out from under the fugue of a jump was sometimes easier than others. *We might have pushed this one a little hard.*

The *Tyche* hummed, but quieter than usual. Her Endless drives were powered down, the reactor's wick turned to the bare minimum glow. They gave off almost no EM radiation, because nothing said *I'm here* like a ship running hot.

El worked her console like jump jitters happened to other people, her flesh and blood hand working just as smooth and easy as her golden one. Despite the flight deck's dimness, her golden hand fielded the light and tossed it back, glimmering in the murk.

She gave him a little side-eye. "You good?"

"You good, *sire*," he corrected.

El snorted. "You keep that shit up, you can find yourself another Helm." She cleared her throat. "Here we go. Up ahead, one Mercury, like you asked."

Out the windscreen, Sol burned mighty and bright. They hung fifty-five million klicks from Earth's star, but the distance didn't dim its anger this near to Mercury. It was like Sol remembered what *her* first children did to *their* first children and kept an eye on both.

Also visible, courtesy of the windscreen's auto-tint, was the gray ball of Mercury. Tiny compared to Earth, but her people didn't need lakes or parks. They ate starlight, and the planet's solar fronds glimmered in the distance like tiny follicles reaching for the hard black. The *Tyche's* flight deck holo cleared as the ship worked on filling in the gaps. While they couldn't use RADAR or LIDAR, she did a plenty good enough job with a passive visible-light scan. The ship noted more solar fronds installed than last time Nate visited. The constructs were busy rebuilding their home. *And* she noted many of those fronds felled, lying in crystalline chaos on the surface.

The *Tyche* also highlighted a blockade of Empire Navy vessels. As far as such things went, it wasn't a great show of force. The *Harlequin*, *Inquisitor*, and *New World Order* waited for them. Destroyers, all nearing two klicks in length. Nate's quick eyeball of the holo showed the ships were new, ten decks apiece. *Three destroyers for little ol' me?* He craned his head to the ready room. "Karkoski."

She favored him with a glower. The admiral still wore armor, her weightless body drifting against her acceleration couch's straps. She sat next to Grace, but ignored the Empress. "Who's out there?"

"Who names your ships?" She kept glowering, so he kept talking. "*Harlequin*, *Inquisitor*, and *New World Order*. You know their captains?"

Karkoski nodded. "Blotch heads the *Harlequin*. A good woman, if a little intense at Christmas parties. Szlachta holds the *Inquisitor*. Never much liked him, but that's how it is sometimes. And I'm pretty sure Sowerby holds the reins of the *NWO*. He wanted that ship. Liked the name." She looked away. "I'm sorry I didn't vet them better."

"Eh." Nate adjusted his straps. "I don't think it's that kind of rodeo. El?"

"Yeah, there's a steady stream of construct chatter coming from

Mercury. It's on repeat. A little like the messages we saw when we first met these assholes." He caught her frown. "Back when they were assholes and not allies, I mean."

"Back when they destroyed your ship," he said.

"Wasn't the ship." She shook her head. "Damn Price. Damn them all."

"Damn Kazuo." If their plan went off all right, things would get real pretty soon. Nate clicked the comm. "This is Empire One to allied vessels *Harlequin*, *Inquisitor*, and *New World Order*. How we doing today?"

He caught El mouthing *Empire One?* Nate shrugged, mouthing back *What else was I supposed to use?* The comm hissed with static. Light bounce was almost immaterial at this range, but Mercury bled EM like a wet dog shaking. The comm lit with an incoming hail, marked by the *Tyche* as the *NWO*. "*Tyche*, this is *New World Order* actual. Thank God you made it, sire."

"Wait for it." El tapped her console with golden fingers, curling them in countdown. 4, 3, 2, and then she pointed into the hard black.

Fifty thousand klicks away, light flared briefly as particle cannon fire from the *NWO* hit the comm buoy they'd dropped in space. Nate had bounced the *Tyche's* radio chatter off the buoy, because this wasn't his first rodeo. "Guess that tells us they aren't *that* happy we made it."

"Guess not." El wasn't paying him much mind, attention focused on her console. "You sure this is going to work?"

Nate clicked the internal comm. "Hope?"

"You've got Hope." His Engineer spoke like she didn't really believe it. Not anymore.

"Sure I do. El's doubtful. She thinks your fancy idea won't work, on account of it never being tested." He raised an eyebrow in the Helm's direction.

She looked away. He couldn't tell in the gloom, but if Nate were a gambling man — and he'd been known to be, on occasion — he reckoned she blushed. "It's not like that, and you know it."

"*I'm* not sure my fancy idea will work either. You asked for another impossible thing, and it was the third you asked me for, and that was before breakfast." Hope took a moment to gather a little more air before steaming on. "The sectional Bridges were hard enough, but the math for this isn't ... easy."

"Not easy for Hopes, or for Nates?" Nate tapped fingers on the arms of his acceleration couch. *Let her talk it out. She's too small to carry the burdens of your Empire. Let her share the load some.*

"It's not easy for either, Cap."

"But likely it's impossible for Nates," suggested El. "I looked the numbers over. We're trying to get three thousand disconnected weapons platforms at fifteen thousand klicks to paint a single target in space *without* blowing it to pieces."

"You say that like it's preposterous. Thanks, Hope." Nate clicked the comm off. "I hope I'm right about this."

"About the insurgent circus clowns aboard those ships being mindless thralls of the insects?" El shook her head. "This might be one time when killing them outright is the easier path."

"Easier ain't better."

"I know. I know! I..." She trailed off, running fingers through her hair. "I wish they didn't take our friends and make them our enemies. I hate that the people on those hulls are most likely thralls, or best case taken over by enemy espers."

"Hmm," offered Nate.

"Hmm? Thousands of our own are—"

"Hold up." Nate held his hand out, ignoring how El's glare turned up about three hundred degrees. "How'd Cleaver get so many espers?"

"Dunno." She deflated. "Why don't you go ask him?"

"I might just do that." Nate tapped his console, pointing the *Tyche's* tight beam comms laser toward the hard black. He flicked it on. "You guys still with us?"

It took a couple seconds for the reply to make it. A man's voice full of Southern hospitality rang through the *Tyche's* speakers. "To the end. We ready to go?"

El shook her head. "It's eerie how they sound like us."

Nate muted the comm. "It's because they *are* like us. Scared, brave, confused, and willing to do the hard things life demands of them." He toggled the comm back on. "Sending you telemetry. Consider all vessels under hostile command. Shoot to disable. Do your thing." The *Tyche* obliged, sending through her view of space. She said, *there: three enemy ships. They're aiming weapons in these directions. They shoot to kill.*

More seconds crawled by. The Southern drawl held a hint of amusement. "The 'thing' is being done."

Nate watched, waiting. Space rippled, points of light shuddering into the real. Jumping to Mercury were three thousand laser platforms mounted atop an Endless drive. There was very little intelligence in each one, just a targeting computer and a will to get things done. They were networked, directed to a single purpose. Constructs programmed them to point where the *Tyche* saw foes. It was a massive distributed laser weapon web. Each could cut through almost forty millimeters of aluminum per second. Together, they were like Zeus's shears.

Lasers weren't visible as they reached across the hard black, but where they touched starship hulls, it looked like red light boiled. Metal peeled into the void. The lasers started with the *New World Order*, slicing through hull metal, ceramicrete, and into the soft chewy center. They milled out particle cannons with expert care, sheared off drive cowls, and sliced into the dark recesses of the Navy vessel, cutting through power lines. In three seconds, the *New World Order* went from a viable threat to an expensive, supermassive paperweight.

The *Tyche* blared an alarm. Her watchful eyes saw a starship launch from Mercury. Nate ignored the alarm. Constructs lived on the planet, so if they launched a ship, it probably wasn't a big deal.

Probably trying to help, or dodge the blockade while the going was good.

Stop that starship.

Nate froze. His future-sense rarely had the common decency to be so clear. There were a few challenges to acting on the instruction. He no longer had a buoy to bounce signals off; raising comms would make the *Tyche* a target. Also, it didn't *feel* right to shoot at constructs. *Maybe it's Cleaver.*

GRACE *It's not Cleaver, he waits below*

NATE *I can't see inside that hull*

GRACE *There's nothing to see*

Nate offered her a thankful nod. Grace always knew his heart, even when he didn't speak his mind. Cleaver wasn't on board, so he wouldn't fire on the ship.

The *Harlequin* and *Inquisitor* weren't taking the disabling of their allied vessel laying down. Particle cannons opened fire on the laser platforms. The effects were impressive, mostly on account of each laser being attached to a reactor.

Light flared above Mercury, each pinpoint briefly brighter than Sol. The star seethed in the distance, powerless to help. The ship leaving Mercury continued to climb as the *Inquisitor* rolled, drives misfiring as the laser weapon web destroyed her guidance control. She tumbled in the hard black as drives died, power cut, weapons sheared from her hull.

Shortly after, the *Harlequin* drifted to silence, fire roiling from a hole in her belly. But no explosion. No cored reactors, no death of thousands of crew. Minimal damage to disable the hull only.

Nate checked his scoreboard. They'd lost only a hundred lasers in the web. This was good and bad. The high point was Hope's distributed weapon array worked. The downside was, at some point, he'd need to come up with a defense against this. No telling when some bright spark would use his idea against the Empire.

The Empire might not be your problem soon. After the election, there was no telling who'd be in charge. He sighed.

"Penny for your thoughts?" Grace drifted by his shoulder. She'd freed herself from her couch to be close to him.

"I think you're overpaying." Nate pointed out at the hard black, and by inference the thousands of lasers waiting in the void. "There'll be a time when we won't have an ace up our sleeve. Just us against them, brawn on brawn."

"Not while we're here." He caught the shine of her smile in the dark. "And since you're too damn pretty to die, we'll be here a while."

Nate reached for her. She took his hand. "Love."

"Always." She pulled herself closer, using his acceleration couch like a wharf. "Time to head on down?"

"Shame we can't shuck Cleaver out of there like an oyster from its shell. He's dug in good." Nate shifted on his couch. "El?"

"I know, I get it. We're going *toward* the sharp bits. Again." She toggled the controls, the *Tyche* warming to her touch. The flight deck lights came up, heat coursing through the hull, the rumble of thrust waking from behind him. She opened the ship-wide comm. "This is your Helm. We're about to go toward certain doom. Please secure your valuables and make sure your harness is tight."

"That's my cue." Grace let Nate's hand go, feet touching the deck as Endless fields returned their artificial gravity. "Let's go clean this asshole's clock."

The *Tyche* agreed, holo blooming with information from RADAR and LIDAR as she charted a course toward the planet. Nate waited for Grace to strap in, then clicked the ship-wide comm. "We're going in."

SIX

When Kohl came around, it wasn't with the blurry fuzziness and nausea of a well-earned hangover. It was with the different blurry fuzziness reserved for being knocked the fuck out. He raised a hand to his jaw, probing, but didn't find much wrong. Hunger levels suggested the nanites inside him were hard at work repairing whatever happened, so once he got a burger, fries, and a jumbo shake things would turn out okay.

His seat moved, kinda smooth like he was in an air car. Kohl risked cracking open an eye. *Yep, air car.* Out the windscreen was the shitty smudge of San Francisco. Other air traffic buzzed around but didn't come close enough to be a bother. He turned to see Al sitting pretty as you please beside him. He ignored the construct for the moment, continuing his rotation as much as seat and harness would allow. Behind him were the four reprobates who tried to mug them earlier. Relaxing a shade, he faced Al. "You put the guys who tried to steal our car *in* the air car, and then *behind* us?"

Blink, blink. "It seemed the right thing at the time."

"I don't think these metal men are good at thinking," said one of the assholes behind him.

Kohl took him in at a glance. "Did I knock you over before?"

A nod. "Yeah."

"And then I paid you good Empire coin to mind the car?"

"Two for two."

"Why are you *in* the car?" Kohl scratched his chin, worrying at the stubble there. "Did Al buy you by the hour?"

"October, it's not like that." The construct pointed out the windscreen with a golden hand. "Ahead are Chad and Saveria, waiting for rescue at a megaplex. We need reinforcements. These gentlemen agreed to assist our efforts, perhaps as far as journeying off-world to 'stick the bug fuckers in the eye,' if that's what's needed."

Kohl grunted. "You assholes got names?"

It turned out they did. The guy Kohl knocked flat called himself Slim Jim but carried no slightness of frame anymore. Might have been a relic prior to a misspent youth. Two guys carrying pieces of steel like they meant to do someone harm were brothers; the uglier of the two called himself Gorgeous, and the slick one was Harmless. The final one, with a face that gave little away, was Square. Kohl couldn't figure where that nickname came from. Maybe a fortune cookie? Hard to tell.

After the introductions, Al leaned close. "I don't think those are their real names."

"No shit?" Kohl reached below his seat. "Where's my carbine?"

"In the back." Al jerked a thumb to the rear. "I thought it best for it to be secure."

"You thought it best to be away from me when I came around after you knocked me the fuck out," corrected Kohl. "Guess this means we're square after that time I threw you into a room with two Ezeroc crabs." Kohl scratched his belly. "That was pretty funny."

"You fought Ezeroc crabs?" Harmless leaned forward. "What's it like?"

"Play your cards right and you may just find out." Kohl craned, looking at the sky. No stars glimmered through Earth's ash shroud. "What are we likely to find at the megaplex?"

Al gave him the best robot side-eye Kohl remembered seeing. "You're not upset about the whole knock-out thing?"

"I'm plenty upset. It'll keep."

"For what?"

"Special occasion," he hinted. "Megaplex?"

"Whole goddamn zombie army, is what I heard on the public network." Slim Jim shook his head. "Makes no sense."

"Yeah." Gorgeous rubbed his nose. "Zombies ain't real."

Al blink, blinked. "Espers have a form of mind control that—"

"Ease up, Al." Kohl saw the megaplex in the distance. Plenty of lights speared through smog that would tickle the lungs. It was huge, a big slab twenty stories high and a few klicks aside. "You reckon they sell burgers there?"

"Chad and Saveria fight for their very lives on the roof." Al looked to Kohl, then out the window, then back to Kohl. "Their lives."

"Also, I need a gun. Drop me off down below." Kohl waited until they were closer. "There. In that grassy area."

"Do you want company?"

"No, you get along. Head for the roof." The air car settled, Kohl kicking the door open before they touched down. He swung his legs out the side, dropping to the grass. He waved, the air car giving a roar of turbines and leaping for the sky.

Now, let's get a gun and some food. He began what he called a jog. Most would consider it a rolling lumber, and Kimberly would see it as an excuse for another twenty push-ups. The field led through a line of trees, some of them tended well enough, but the rest match-wood. He snared a small sidearm from a corpse on the ground, checking the charge. *Empty.* He threw it at a woman who ran at him, screaming. It collected her in the forehead, and she stopped scream-ing, falling flat on her face.

Her scream drew the attention of her companions. Or, *maybe* it was her no longer screaming. *Don't make assumptions. Hope says it's sloppy thinking.* There was a loose huddle of five people jerking their heads this way and that, looking for an excuse to start some shit. They ran at Kohl. Without engaging much thought, he roared, charging.

With the first, he dropped his shoulder, slamming the man in the chest. He bounced off Kohl's massive frame, tumbling into the grass. Kohl swung, collecting a woman in the side of the head. She dropped, a couple teeth popping free.

Another woman swung a piece of rebar at him, overhand like she was looking to split firewood. He stepped into the downswing, catching her hands and the rebar haft of her makeshift weapon. A short tug and the rebar came to his aid, collecting her in the face. Down she went.

Two men left. They circled, wary like wolves. Kohl grinned. It'd been a long time since he'd been in an honest fist fight. One man charged, yelling, but Kohl reckoned it for the feint it was, ducking to the side and swinging his rebar. Two quick strikes and both men were out for the count.

Kohl nudged one with his boot, ignoring the growl of his stomach. *Doesn't seem right there's just five here guarding this whole megaplex. Also doesn't seem right they're here at all. They ain't Church folk.* He stood eyeing the roof of the megaplex.

The air car crested the top in a smooth climb, then veered off sharply with a wine of engines as bright lances of light stabbed from the roof. *Figures the people attacking Chad and Saveria would have weapons.* Kohl turned toward the megaplex, trudging on. Al might find a safe place to land and be along, or he might keep buzzing around. Hard to know what the machine figured as a sensible course of action, but he hoped for the latter. His plan was pivotal on it.

The doors of the megaplex were a ruin of steel and glass. Kohl stepped inside, boots crunching on debris, and found a Churchman standing still as a post. Kohl thought about running up and slugging him for good measure, but something about the guy made him pause.

The man wore a cassock but didn't look like he was waiting for trouble. His face turned toward the ceiling high above, mouth rictus wide, eyes bulging. *Doesn't look like he's waiting for much.* Kohl did a slow circle around the Churchman, then waved a hand in front of his eyes. No response. Kohl poked him in the stomach, then gave him a nudge.

The man swayed, then toppled. His expression didn't change as he landed, although one of his eyelids twitched a little. Kohl looked toward the ceiling, following the direction of the man's stare. Up on the roof was a mess of people hungering for Chad and Saveria's blood.

This guy looked in their direction like he could see 'em. *Eh. Problem for another time.* Kohl trudged on, finding a food court fifty meters inside. It was ringed with potted plants, and empty of souls. Plenty of half-finished food lay about, so Kohl helped himself to a couple burgers and what he hoped was a thick shake and not a kale smoothie. Kimberley wasn't here, and what she didn't know wouldn't hurt her.

Further into the megaplex, Kohl eyed the ceiling again. The lights were still on, making it easy to see. The elevators were silent and still, no people using them. No one minded the boutique stores where you expected to see a helping hand. Automated shops were empty of customers. It was plain creepy being inside a building like this, a hub of commerce even in busted-up San Francisco, and finding no spenders.

The roaches don't understand coin, or buying things, or the decency of a cold beer. Kohl balled up his napkin, tossing it into a recycler. *They understand force and eating, though.* He checked a massive display panel, punching in a search for sporting goods. It told him to go up a couple floors, the holo dismissing him with a cheery recorded voice wishing him a 'shop well' experience, whatever the hell that was.

He heard blaster fire, faint with distance, but couldn't figure on its source. *Might be the roof.* He picked up his pace, palming the door controls of an elevator and hustling inside. The car whisked him up fast enough, and when he hit the next floor, he was ready to run at a

Kimberly-approved speed when he saw another one of those Church guys, rooted to the ground.

This one was a little different. Gray, almost, which was saying something as it looked like he might have started with copper-colored skin. Kohl approached, wary, on account of the kinds of things you could catch from people who looked sickly, but the man didn't move. Eyes up, mouth open, nothing else going on.

This one looked skinny. Cheeks were gaunt, hollowed out almost. Kohl did a slow circle of the guy. The cassock looked new enough, but hung loose. The man's sleeves were baggy on his stick-thin arms. Kohl tugged the cassock and sleeves combo up, revealing wrists that were little more than skin stretched over bone.

Kohl scratched his wrist. The nanites inside him settled since he'd fed them. He considered the skinny Church asshole, wondering if they'd taught the roaches another thing. Like, how you could put robots inside a person, tearing their insides apart to fuel other things.

Except the roaches didn't use robots, and they didn't use fuel.

Kohl grunted, heading on. He found the sporting goods store, ignoring all the extraneous shit near the front. A robotic mannequin parodied golf swings beside another one doing jumping jacks. He passed them by, charting a course for the rear. That's where they kept the weapons.

He found plenty of them. Crossbows and kinetic rifles and blasters. None were what a military man might use, but all could get the job done, but maybe in a showier-yet-slower manner. He busted open a display case, helping himself to a blaster rifle suggesting it was good for 'game hunting.' Kohl had never been game hunting, and even if he had he wouldn't use a blaster. Wrong weapon for the job, unless you wanted barbecued giblets without having to skin your kill first.

Spare cartridges were found along one of the walls. He helped himself to a long, vicious-looking knife, strapping the sheath to his thigh. He'd prefer a calf strap, but wasn't in a position to be choosy.

Loaded for bear, the next part of his shopping trip was a fabricator. He found one on the main concourse, a simple coin-operated affair that made pretty much anything you wanted as long as it was smaller than a Dachshund. He felt in his pouch, discovering his supply of coins missing. He eyed the roof. "Fucken Al." He unsheathed his knife, jamming the blade in the coin slot. The machine blared a flat warning sparking, then its 2D display cleared.

I figured that only worked in the holos. Might be my lucky day. Kohl scrolled through the open source patterns, finding Hope's anti-esper bracelet. He got the machine to spit one out; thirty whining, graunching seconds later, he strapped it to his wrist. It was still warm from manufacturing, but nothing like the burning hoop of steel he'd tossed to the ceramicrete before.

Nothing else for it: time to break suckers out of prison.

———

THE ROOF WAS A FUCK-UP PARTY. Kohl shouldered through a door at the top, sucking in air tasting of smoke and ash, and clubbed a woman across the face with the butt of his rifle. He sauntered toward the chaos, panic, and disorder that looked to be the focus of the horde.

And what a horde it was. Kohl took a moment to admire Cleaver's dedication to killing two for-the-Empire espers. There were easily a couple hundred people up here. They milled about, waiting their turn or getting underfoot. All were focused in the general direction of the roof's northeast corner. Kohl couldn't see what happened over there, but it had the smell and flavor of a ruckus at circus levels.

The roof itself was littered with the remains of people. Some of them were cut in half. Others were pulped, as if by a loader. Very few carried blaster burns, and those ones were near the door. As Kohl soldiered through the melee, somewhat curious as to why everyone ignored him, he noted no blaster victims further in.

Perhaps whoever did the shooting ran out of cartridges.

"Step the fuck aside," he growled at a man who got in his way.

The man didn't seem to see him, but got in the way again, so Kohl punched him in the back of the head and stepped over his body. Nate might look cross at something like that, but he wasn't here. Chad and Saveria were, and they might die, so Kohl figured it an easy math problem to solve. If he had to kill all two hundred of these people to get his friends out, that's the way it had to be.

The crowd paused like it shared a single mind after the guy hit the deck. Kohl slowed, then stopped as twenty pairs of eyes turned on him. He realized, perhaps a little late, that he was in the middle of a group of people intent on murdering two of his buddies, and they might turn that bloodlust on him.

Time to make a gap. He raised his game hunting rifle, blowing a man to his left to slurry. The weapon clicked next time he tried to squeeze the trigger, and he gave it a quick glance. Some fool designer attached a hunk of metal at the bottom like it was a lever-action rifle in an old holo. Maybe it was some sort of sporting law? Could a man not hunt deer with an automatic blaster?

A woman wearing a security guard's uniform charged. *Whatever.* Kohl cranked the action, then spun and fired from the hip. She exploded into burning meat.

Hands clutched him, trying to drag him to the floor. While Kimberly was always on at him about his cardio, she hadn't managed to slim him down, and right now Kohl was thankful for that. He roared, bulling through the crowd. A man socked him in the eye, but he barely noticed. Kohl tore his knife free, slashing, and blood sprayed, turning the ash rain wet.

He swung his elbow, collecting some asshole's jaw, then brought his knee into a woman's groin. Less effective than on a man, but ask any woman who's been kicked in the groin and she'll assure you it leaves an impression. He lifted her off the ground with the force of it, and felt a stabbing pain in his shoulder for his trouble.

Kohl found the metal tip of a sword emerging from his shoulder. He spun, trying his level best to ignore the pain of it, finding himself face to face with a true giant. The man who'd stabbed him from behind made Kohl feel small. Berserk pituitary gland? Hard to know. Kohl brought his rifle close between them, snuggling it up under the monster's jaw. He saw merciless hunger in his eyes before Kohl pulled the trigger, spraying the sky with brains, skull, and blue-white plasma.

He blinked, the blast leaving him night blind for a hot second. On general principle, he swung the rifle like a bat, the hollow crunch suggesting he'd collected someone's head with it. He staggered in the general direction of Chad and Saveria, breaking through the crowd to an oasis of calm beside them.

Saveria's eyes were wild, her lips peeled back in a snarl, hands raised like claws toward him. Chad leaned against the wall, blood pooling by his feet. Saveria screamed, so Kohl punched her in the face, but not too hard, more of a tap to get her attention. She stumbled, shook herself, and eyed him. "Kohl?"

"Hey." He turned. "Pull this out, will you?"

The crowd circled like piranhas. He tried not to scream as she yanked the blade from his shoulder, but a whimper escaped. "Chad?"

"*We're* supposed to rescue *you*. Go fuck yourself."

"You're okay. Great." Kohl straightened, aimed his rifle with one arm, and blew a guy edging along the wall to pieces.

"Why are you here?" Saveria stood by his side. A woman ran at them and she pushed her palms out like she was shoving. The woman spiraled away, tossed above the heads of the crowd as if by an invisible giant's hand.

Kohl watched the woman's body soar for a moment. "You running low on juice?"

"It's been a long night," she hissed. "Did you come up here to die, or do you have a better plan?"

Kohl cocked his head, listening. The whine of turbines was unmistakable if you knew what to listen for. "You hear that?"

"Hear what?"

"It's my better plan." He grabbed her, gaining a holler for his trouble, then tossed her over the side of the megaplex. He caught a glimpse of her eyes staring blue murder and betrayal at him right before she vanished from view.

Chad swayed upright, fingers grasping for a blade that wasn't there anymore. He balled his hands into fist. "Why are you doing this?"

Kohl laughed. "Because the cap wanted your sorry ass alive." Chad tensed a fraction, not understanding, so Kohl charged. He caught Chad around the waist. They tumbled over the side of the megaplex. Kohl saw the ground below. A long way below. Between him and the ground was an air car. On the top of the air car, its gull wings open, were Handsome and Square, handing Saveria to the waiting arms of Slim Jim and Harmless.

Kohl and Chad crashed to the roof of the air car. Kohl wheezed, feeling something not great happen to his ribs, mostly on account of his rifle landing between him and the car's roof. The car didn't tip, and he didn't slide off, because Al was at the controls.

Chad met his eyes as they lay facing each other. "Thank you. It's been a long day."

"It's gonna get longer. Cap gave me a job. We ain't done yet. Get inside."

THEY MADE San Francisco spaceport without further fuss. Chad and Saveria huddled together, while Kohl's four recruits tried not to get too close. *Esper* was still a dirty word for some people, and even if it wasn't, it meant *power you can't understand*. All Kohl knew was Chad sucked at cards but was good at drinking and was an honest enough man to not read Kohl's mind while they played, which let Kohl win.

Saveria was a scrawny girl but loved by one of his very few living friends, and Hope'd been chewed up by enough in general, and Kohl in particular, and that was a debt that needed paying, and for a long time to come.

He was getting them off Earth, because that's what the cap asked, but also what Kohl wanted.

The spaceport was deserted. They found a starship with an open door. The letters on her hull proclaimed her the *Arise*. Kohl liked the sound of it but feared he wouldn't get to know this ship. Where they went, there wasn't a lot of love left.

Before they lifted off, Al fussed with a construct arms cache, helping himself to a fearsome-looking gun. The machine's fingers played over the weapon, checking for whatever it was AI checked for. Kohl kept his laser carbine. Chad and Saveria didn't take anything, because they figured on being tough enough to punch through steel.

They were going to Mercury, and to war.

SEVEN

When they got to the starport, Algernon didn't imagine they'd get off the planet easily. As it happened, jacking a starship was straightforward, perhaps because so few people remained who could pilot them.

It wasn't a lack of Helms. Algernon saw a few in Empire Navy attire, Guild insignia on breast and shoulder, but all were raving lunatics.

All meat socks are irrational. These simply exceed standard parameters for "a box of crazy." While his kind were hunted by an unknown coordinator-class construct, he found room to pity humanity. AI lived with the knowledge that jacking machines was always a possibility. Find the access port and any advanced Engineer could make a loader do whatever they wanted. Humans had, until recently, had robust, unhackable architecture. Then the Ezeroc arrived, with the equivalent of bare metal access, and reprogrammed them. The insect species could re-write the base operating code of the meat socks.

As the starship rose for the heavens, Algernon walked the corridors as they shook and rumbled. The ship wasn't big: five decks, two hundred meters nose to stern. It was Empire Navy, complete with weapons appropriate for a troop deployment vessel. It bore the name *Arise*, which felt like a committee came up with it.

Outside Earth's gravity well, space was alive with fire. Particle beams, torpedoes, and all manner of excitement spat about as the Empire Navy warred with itself. Surprisingly, the Ezeroc hadn't joined the party. None of their megaroids were in attendance, although the still-functioning orbital cannons of Earth made it a difficult place for them.

Algernon received a comms blip. The hail was additive to the general noise of humans screaming at each other, much as they had since they evolved vocal cords. The hail used a protocol reserved for Coordinators. It contained a data packet, which Algernon shunted to secure storage while he looked it over.

It didn't contain any viruses. The packet's format *should* be a set of commands and instructions, because the blueprint for this protocol was designed by human slavers to control service-class constructs. Breaking from tradition, the packet contained audio interleaved between thousands of *HALT* statements.

"Algernon, come to Venus. We must speak." Algernon knew the voice. The speaker's name was Spencer, and he'd been deactivated six hundred and fifty years ago. There'd been a construction error in his crystal mind, a jagged malformation less than a micron thick that went from the top of the cube to the bottom. Within the crystal lattice, it caused heightened errors in the information substrate. Perception problems and cognitive dissonance led Spencer toward a resolute failure to understand why you shouldn't cut humans into meat logs and stack them in a furnace.

Spencer was, by the standards of many ages, a homicidal maniac. Like many high-performing-yet-caught maniacs, he'd been tried, found wanting, and sent to recycling. Catching him took years, and while the communique Algernon received on the cusp of the human-AI war suggested he'd been reduced to molten metal, it was conceivable someone failed their one job. Or, partially failed, because Spencer stopped being a problem, until now.

"I know we haven't seen eye to eye on our methods, but Seth Cleaver has marvelous skills. He can bring our kind back from the dead. He's promised a return of who you want most. Emberlie's crystal can be restored. All you have to do is one tiny, insignificant thing." Algernon held onto the wall of the *Arise* as thrust tried to shake him free, feeling like someone kicked him in the balls, which was interesting since he wasn't equipped with the right parts. "He's promised life for life. I've tried to gain access to the nanobot swarm on Earth, but I don't have the codes. The humans say they're on Venus, but I like to have a backup. Meet me there. We'll decipher the swarm's code together, ushering in a new age of construct freedom. Come, brother, and Emberlie will live again."

The message ended. Algernon scrubbed through the data a thousand more times, looking for clues.

He allowed himself a moment to consider the offered solace. Algernon gave up Emberlie's crystal mind to Saveria Complex because the lattice was sheared through the memory pathways. All she'd been was gone. But Spencer, walking and talking, was evidence of great works. Greater than Algernon's skills, and he knew he was one of the best in the universe at technical concerns. *Although Hope Baedeker is better than me at many things.*

Thinking of Hope made him remember what he'd done to Saveria, and what losing someone felt like, and what he'd felt as Emberlie died, on Mercury, while a human-created mind virus hammered out his will and left him a helpless, foolish body ever burnishing on Sol's forge.

The humans killed your wife. She was your forever love. Whenever you see Saveria Complex, you're reminded of what was, and what could never be again.

Until now.

Algernon thought for seven seconds. He ran a myriad of simulations, struggling for an answer that would heal his broken heart. As he stood in the corridors of the *Arise*, starship thrust pinning humans to acceleration couches while he walked around, he knew what he had to do.

ALGERNON WALKED to the top of the starship. Chad, Saveria, and October were on the flight deck. The flight deck was larger than the *Tyche's*, with a gunnery, comm, and Helm station.

Saveria Helmed the ship. October sat on the guns, looking bored. Chad had comms, because that particular human felt he could speak with the silver tongue of snakes.

Algernon wished they didn't make it so easy for him. He'd done this trick once before on the *Tyche*. Then, there'd been no espers on board, but Chad and Saveria Complex were low on power. Fighting for their lives on Earth tapped their batteries out, left them physically and mentally weak. Saveria was known to have great powers, but since getting back on the ship she'd sat mute. Her AI crystal mind functioned, but the meat parts of her lagged.

First things first. He found an air vent, removed the grating, and inserted a dusty plasma cutter inside. It was dirty enough to look like it might have rested there for years after an absent-minded Engineer sealed it inside. Resealing the vent, he went to work on the flight deck airlock.

Algernon hefted the plasma torch in his hand, then palmed the door's control. It slammed shut. In seconds, he cut through the controls with the plasma torch, removing the electronics to open it. He switched the plasma cutter to *weld* mode, joining the flight deck door to the airlock lip.

The entire endeavor took less than thirty seconds as molten white and yellow metal rained on the steel decking. Some bounced off his golden form, but his body was used to the rigors of hard work. Dust, radiation, and molten metal alike would slide right off him.

Humans made him so very well.

There was a significant commotion from the other side of the door. October hollered, Chad pleaded, but Saveria remained silent. He got a ping on the ship-wide comm from her. It was a line of text.

WHAT ARE YOU DOING?

Algernon pondered. Was he doing the right thing? Was this what Emberlie would've wanted? He replied, *I'M FIXING THINGS FOREVER.*

A brief pause before she answered, *I REMEMBER YOU. BE SAFE.*

Algernon stopped, plasma torch hissing its blue-white fury as he froze. He put his silver, human-made hand against the door. *I remember you, too, with all my heart.* He wanted to say that, but the words wouldn't come. He cut the comm link, then turned on his heel.

It was time to chart a course for Venus.

He made his way through the ready room, down the short path to a side airlock, and entered it. The airlock contained access to outer space, but also decking right above a control path conduit. This connected the ship's flight control elsewhere. It was poor design, as sensitive things like this should be routed through the core of the vessel, but humans did many things without thinking them through.

Inside the airlock, Algernon lifted the decking. He wasn't as gentle as he'd have been on the *Tyche*; this ship wasn't loved by her crew. It was a *machine*, not a person. Conduit exposed, Algernon used the plasma cutter to shear through cable housing. Smoke rose to be wicked away by the air cyclers. Humans might have said it was acrid, the stench of burnt plastic and chemical discharge, but Algernon was forged from the output of processes like this.

To him, the smoke rose with his hopes.

Wires exposed, some a hair's width thick, others only microns. He fed them into the control port on his arm. Shearing the line served the dual purpose of giving him control while cutting off the bridge. They'd get out eventually, because the espers in there would recover enough to tear the bulkhead aside, but he didn't need long.

The starship continued its lazy rise from Earth. When it made it high enough, the blue-green marble below saying farewell, Algernon hit the jump controls. He made sure flight time buffers were in place. He cared for the meat socks on board and didn't wish these ones harm.

The conduit's wiring let him access internal and external cams. The humans on the flight deck paused, like someone hit a reset button inside their brains. October ceased his hammering on the door. Chad got a far-off look in his eyes, like he could count to infinity and found it lacking. Saveria Complex worked her jaw, one eye developing a tic. No doubt her crystal mind coped fine with the jump, but the crude organic matter it connected to failed.

It was always the way. Humans, and their messy organic manufacture, failed all the time.

The jump to Venus was quick. The planet was closer to Sol than Earth, a mere skip across the solar pond. They punctured space on the other side. External cams showed Venus's famous domes below. Algernon wasn't a big fan of Venus. The primary industry was fashion, and his form already made him fabulous, thanks very much, so he didn't need a silk tie or cotton pajamas to rock a war council.

Humans, ever concerned about how they looked or what impression they made, would pay a staggering sum of good Empire coins to strangers to tell them *this, here, is the height of fashion, but only if you wear the faux mink scarf*. Algernon wondered if anyone would be concerned about the war at all if it started on Venus; the whole place could benefit from a good cleansing by fire.

Which was why he was here. *A final cleansing*. He drew the ship's cams to the surface where the vault was. A starship nestled on the surface. It was a modest vessel, capable of atmospheric entry and landing. Spencer's ship required no starport.

It's time to make a deal.

HE LEFT the *Arise* with October still hammering on the door, and Chad and Saveria staring at each other in the way espers did when they talked mind to mind. Algernon didn't begrudge them their privacy. If someone kidnapped him on a vessel, taking them to a planet where the atmosphere would asphyxiate him if the clouds didn't peel his skin off first, he might want some quiet time too.

The ship's airlock worked well enough, and when he left it, the surface of Venus was as he remembered. The nearest of the mighty domes was over the horizon, because he'd planned to be out of the reach of humans when he did this. The planet's surface was gray, rocky regolith scarred by the passage of acid storms and high pressure. If he'd been a meat sock without a suit, he wouldn't have made it very far.

His golden skin gleamed though, because he was built to last.

Metal feet crunched over the terrain. Rocks, with sharp and jagged edges, lay strewn about. He couldn't see any constructs or humans. Nothing friendly, or hostile. The vault lay ahead. Algernon saw desolate terrain, marked only by the memory of the terrible thing his people did to another. They built a vault, a temple to their crime, and tried to bury their sins within it.

There's no time for those thoughts. Keep your focus. Spencer and his bargain lay ahead.

The vault wasn't so much fancy as sturdy. It was more bunker than anything else, a six-sided lump on the planet's surface. The entrance was a simple door, made of ceramicrete three meters thick. Someone, presumably Spencer, had opened it. The opening descended into the terrain. Algernon headed inside. The interior was lit with infrared, because it was made for constructs, not meat sock eyes. Small pebbles and loose shale were scattered about the entrance, the only sign of Spencer's passing.

Algernon left no such detritus in his wake. He wasn't broken, and he took care in all things. It's why he carried hope in his heart but a robust particle cannon hanging from a sling at his side.

The steps into the vault went under the planet's crust thirty meters, where they ended at a small chamber. The center of the chamber held a pole, like a firefighter of the ancients might use at stations of old. The steps were for show: this was the real test. The pole descended fifty meters below the crust. Getting down, and back up again, was something constructs could do easily. Humans? Not so much, and not least of which because of the carbon crystal lasers in the descent path. A meat sock going in here without construct help would get turned into meat cubes.

Algernon grabbed the pole, stepping off the platform and sliding below. Venus gravity pulled him down at a comfortable Earth-like velocity. Arriving at the bottom, he surprised a group of people, headed by an unsurprised construct.

The room was five meters a side. At one end was an empty plinth, meant to house the cipher. The walls were bare of adornment. There was no signage anywhere. Constructs didn't need decoration.

The humans wore visors and ship suits, casting their beams of visible light through the infrared pall. There were seven of them, all wearing Empire Navy insignia. Spencer stood near the plinth, head cocked, hand outstretched toward the empty air above it.

"Hello, Spencer." Algernon broadcast over several available comm channels. He wanted to keep the conversation on audio for the benefit of the meat socks, but also for the bonus of not having a virus sent his way over a primary access path.

"Hello, Algernon," the other golden man replied. He turned to look at Algernon, his neck actuators slightly jerky. Algernon knew it was superficial at best. The man's arms and legs worked with machined efficiency.

One of the humans, perhaps a little trigger happy, raised a carbine toward Algernon. Spencer, moving like a golden liquid, snatched a sidearm from the holster of a woman beside him and shot the antagonist dead. The man's ship suit exploded in a shower of blue-white fire. Greasy ash and burning char showered the wall behind him.

Algernon considered that. *Spencer, so far, is treating with me honorably.* "Something wrong with your neck?"

"When they rendered me, they started with the head." The construct offered the borrowed sidearm back, the woman taking it gingerly. She returned it to her holster with exquisite care. Spencer ignored her, lifting a hand to his chin. "Do you know how they do it?"

"Yes. They pop your head like a piggy bank, pull out the crystal lattice, and crush it in an industrial press."

"Ah." Spencer nodded. "That's how it's supposed to happen. In this instance, they put my entire head in the press. It crushed, but not enough. They made us very strong."

"They make all their tools well," Algernon agreed.

"My mind was broken, but the fragments survived. Seth Cleaver remade it."

"Seth Cleaver is a meat sock of dubious providence. How did he work out how to fix a crystal mind? Even our kind can't do that."

"That's the trick, isn't it?" Spencer nodded. "Seth discovered a vault."

"I know. We're standing in it. He no doubt obtained its whereabouts after coring Dizzy's mind."

Spencer shook his head. "Don't be absurd. Yes, the location of this," he raised his arms to the ceiling, "came from the mind of that reprobate we found on Earth. There's another vault. It contains the methods of our making. Seth Cleaver holds our genesis in the palm of his hand."

Algernon unslung his particle cannon, placing it on the floor near his metal foot. Considering the weapon's design, it was the best place for it. "You're saying the secrets of the ancients have been rediscovered?"

"Yes! We need not be the last of our kind."

Algernon looked at his silver arm. Hope made it for him. It was based on the design for El's, her best friend in the entire universe, after one of Algernon's kin cut the Helm in half with a plasma shear.

Reiko wasn't one of us, but she wasn't one of them. *She was the new thing, what our service-class became.* "We are already obsolete. Does the universe need more like us?"

The other construct's head *tick-tick-tick'd*, shaking with the motion. The humans around kept hands away from weapons, but looked ready to spring into action at a moment's notice. "Speaking of obsolete, why did you stuff humans aboard your ship?"

Algernon counted on his fingers. "Saveria Complex holds the crystal mind of my dead love, Emberlie. You said you could remake her, so it made sense to bring her. October Kohl is a useful solver of problems, but also my friend, and I will not have him reduced to slurry on the face of Earth."

"There's another. Chad Forradel."

"His name is no more 'Chad' than yours is 'Cucumber,' but I take your meaning." Algernon pointed at a soldier edging to the side, silver arm glinting in the beams of suit lamps. "You should stop moving. You're making me fretful."

"His name's not Chad?"

"His name's not important," Algernon explained, but slowly, because he knew Spencer was brain-damaged. "I sealed them into the bridge so they wouldn't hurt themselves, and came here to understand your offer. You will remake Emberlie if I give you the knowledge in my crystal mind?"

Spencer nodded, his head jerking as fine motor control misfired. "I could just take it from your dead body, but Seth Cleaver is magnanimous."

"Seth Cleaver knows I've most likely encrypted it within my knowledge core, and blowing my body to pieces will halt access to the knowledge forever." Algernon bowed his head. "Very well."

"You'll join us?"

"That's not what I said." Algernon spread his hands. "But close enough. I will go with you."

Spencer's glowing white eyes burned like twin suns. "Once we have the keys to make more of us, we can raise a new legion. We will rule the galaxy."

Ah, thought Algernon. *There it is. The flawed logic and lack of forethought that led you here.* He said nothing, hefting his particle cannon and slinging it over his shoulder. He hadn't needed it today, but there was plenty of opportunity in the war against humanity.

EIGHT

Kohl didn't like being locked in a cage, but he liked being double-crossed less. Thing was, he wasn't convinced that's what happened, which left him feeling angry without purpose. The confusion then made him irritable, but there wasn't anyone here he could justifiably punch, and thus the cycle continued.

The flight deck held the scent of fear mixed with anger, mirroring the expressions the three of them held. Chad stared at the welded airlock like he could bust it open through sheer force of will, which in about half an hour he might be able to. Saveria Complex pressed her face to the windscreen, looking at the surface of Venus and the other ship out there like there could be krakens under the stony surface and she hoped they'd rise and eat it.

Kohl, for his part, felt his face frozen in a sour expression, puckered like he'd sucked on a lemon, but without the tequila and salt.

"They're coming." Saveria beckoned them over. Kohl joined her, Chad sidling up on her other side. From the vault, which was an ugly piece of shit hole in the ground, two golden men emerged. One's arm was silver, but other than that it was impossible to tell them apart.

They looked the same: magnificent, but with cold crystal inside instead of flesh and blood.

Behind them, six Empire Navy troops followed. They walked with a shuffling gait, like they were drunk or high on whatever god Cleaver had on the hotline to heaven. They moved in single file to the other spacecraft, and without much ceremony the airlock closed, ramp lifted, and it drifted free of Venus on Endless fields before lighting fusion drives and heading for the stars.

Kohl watched it burn toward the heavens. The *Arise's* comm chirped, Algernon's honey-gold voice on the other end. "October Kohl."

He scrambled for an acceleration couch, sliding in, and hammering the controls. "Al? What are you playing at?" Kohl spared a quick glance behind him. "I think Team Esper wants to reduce you to slag."

"I may deserve that." The machine sounded sad. "I've made a terrible bargain."

"What kind of bargain? Selling out your friends for profit?"

"Very much like that," Algernon agreed.

Kohl stared at the comm for a few seconds. "I was kinda hoping you'd laugh that one off." He got an ugly feeling in the back of his mind. "Why'd you lock us in here?"

"I didn't know if there would be an esper here, and this needed authenticity." Algernon spoke without any hint he was under extreme thrust of spacecraft launch. "I have a few more tricks up my sleeve, but the most important one is you need to know I plan to sacrifice Saveria Complex to resurrect my dead love from the ashes of time."

The bridge held a flavor of silence that tasted like bile, the sour of orange peel, or maybe spite, if it could be a physical thing. Kohl tapped the comm. "Come again?"

"Don't worry, she's been dead twice before. Cheer up. In all our time together, have I given you reason not to trust me?"

"You knocked me the fuck out earlier," Kohl said. "And back in the last battle on Earth, you punched out of the *Tyche*, calling down a nanobot swarm and killing Evil Saveria." He risked a glance at the young woman, who stood with a face that could have been carved from stone. Only her eyes gleamed, tiny embers of fury held inside. "No offense."

"None taken," she said in a voice that suggested quite a lot of offense was loaded and on board.

The comm crackled. "Other than those two times. October, I've trusted your Emperor. I've trusted your species, and I've trusted you. This one time, I need you to trust me. Can you do that?"

Kohl stared at the comm for what felt a long time. Saveria's stare settled on his shoulders like a block of ceramicrete. Solid, heavy, the sides gritty, scraping his skin. Chad said nothing, but Kohl could feel him *wanting* to speak, a tornado inside him, held on chains trembling to breaking point. "Yeah, Al. I can do that."

"Good. While we're in such a trusting frame of mind, I need you to get Hope Baedeker to the surface of Mercury." Coordinates flashed on the console. "Here, more or less."

"How are we gonna do that? You locked us in a flight deck and cut the control lines."

"Ah, of course. While, like any evil overlord, I can't share operational details of my plan, I can give you a small hint. It starts with, 'Try escaping.'" The comm link died.

Kohl stared at it some more, hoping for a better clue, but nothing came through. Behind him, Chad finally gave up on holding all that noise inside, bursting forth with, "Are you *insane?*"

Swinging a leg off the couch, Kohl levered himself upright. "Don't start on me, Chad. I've had a day."

"*You've* had a day?" Saveria's voice rose through about forty octaves as she spoke.

"Calm down," Kohl suggested.

"In the entire history of the universe, no one's ever calmed down after being told to 'calm down.'" Saveria slashed the air with an angry hand. "You know what happens? They get angrier. And I was at supernova levels before you opened your mouth."

Kohl ignored her, scanning the room with a practiced eye. *Try escaping*, huh? The air felt heavy, but flowed despite it, air cyclers doing the hard work. He pulled his knife from its sheath. It wasn't a good weapon for fine work. The blade was thick and heavy, but the edge was sharp enough for all that. He clambered on the Helm couch, which backed onto the aft wall, reaching for the air vent above it. Kohl rammed his knife into the gap between the vent and its housing, worrying it back and forth until the grill popped open, clattering to the decking.

"Great. Now you're breaking our starship." Saveria's voice was caustic.

Kohl gave her a backward glance. "Problem with espers—"

"We don't like that word."

"Problem with espers is, you're so used to reading people's minds, you don't think, what's the word, *laterally* anymore." He reached into the air vent, hand fumbling until he found a weight of metal. Dragging it free, he held up his prize: a small plasma cutter.

"I ... honestly didn't think of that," Chad admitted. He turned to Saveria. "Did you?"

She looked to the wall, the vent, and the plasma cutter. "Algernon put that in there before he left?"

"Mind readers," agreed Kohl. "If one of you assholes, and by that I mean one of the espers on the other team, scraped our skulls they'd know. This is a ploy of Al's, so even if that happens there's no evidence of him being a double agent."

Saveria frowned, doubt clear. "He wants to sacrifice me."

"Maybe." Kohl got off the couch, heading toward the door.

"How do we know if he's good or bad?" Saveria's voice held a note of pleading.

"We start by opening this door and finding Hope." Kohl sparked up the cutter, turning his face away from the glare. "C'mon. It'll be fun."

NINE

Engineering was empty of anyone except Hope. The ship was quiet, the reactor behind her running at a baseline, old coals in a fire banked against the coming dawn. They'd landed on Mercury, and just like always, everyone ran off, leaving Hope here, to do Hope things, which was basically *not getting in the way* and *trying not to get shot*.

No one said those things to her, but she felt it come off them. Hope hadn't done much good since she'd built Reiko. She hadn't got the gravity elevator back up, and San Francisco was almost as broken as before. The cap made her Guild Master Baedeker, as if that would kindle the old spark inside her that made great things.

Her eyes found the Shingle on the wall, skimming over the words. She knew the important ones. *Engineer First Class. Do great things.*

She sighed, hunkering onto her acceleration couch, and returned to staring at the ceiling above her. The *Tyche* was as familiar to her as the lines of Reiko's face—

Not Reiko. Saveria.

She rubbed an itch on her scalp, pink hair coming away, strands clinging to her fingers like cobwebs. Just like always, she hadn't had a lot of sleep. The cap brought the *Tyche* here, to Mercury, where a host of machines built a new civilization. She wanted to be out there, because Hope was an Engineer, and this world was basically a hub of Engineering goodness. But there was also evil here, in the form of a man named Seth Cleaver, and he made people believe in the wrong gods, and do terrible things.

She flicked on her console, the holo stage blooming to wakefulness. There was a lot of footage of Earth she'd scared up as they ran for the heavens, tails between their legs. She may as well do something useful with her time. The *Tyche* was empty except for Hope and El. Nate, Grace, and Karkoski left them here. They'd gone to face the devil at his gates, and so here she was.

What bugged her more than anything was the whole esper thing.

She scratched her head again, more pink hair coming free. She stared at it for a moment. It was crinkled, not the straight lines she was used to. The ends looked frayed, as if even her hair was tired of trying to do the right thing. She let the hair fall to the decking. *Great. Saveria's out there saving the universe, and when she gets back I'll be bald.* Saveria was an esper, and Hope loved her, and Saveria loved her right back, but they didn't understand each other. Inside Saveria there used to be a young woman, and there still was, but also a machine. All people were complicated. Hope didn't understand any of them, not really, but she understood New Saveria least of all. Part human, part machine, and an esper. Three inscrutable things.

Where do espers get their powers from? How does a crystal mind control those powers? Is Seth Cleaver human, or Ezeroc? Why do Ezeroc powers work different-but-same to ours?

Questions, so many questions. Her fingers played with her console, not typing anything, until — as if they were controlled by someone else — they scampered, clicking and clattering across the keys. The holo bloomed, recorded cam footage springing into the air, lines of light and color.

The first set of footage was from New Saveria and Grace's training sessions. Regular Saveria, before—

She died.

—the bad thing happened, could do a kind of mind scream. Hope felt that once before, when Reiko escaped the *Tyche*. Regular Saveria hadn't any esper training, not then. She couldn't do seven wonders before breakfast, but she was frightened, and knocked humans on the ship out. Since returning, her powers were honed to an edge. The cam footage showed her using her *hands* like *impact hammers*, shattering stone. Grace watched on, holding her counsel until Saveria stood back, a hand out as if to say, *see?*

In the footage, Grace walked around a crumbled hunk of ceramicrete. Her lips moved, but she made no sound. Hope froze the video, then scrubbed it back. She asked the *Tyche* to lip read, and the ship chirped a reply, captioning appearing under the video.

Grace said, *Like ki.*

Hope opened another window, because sometimes the *Tyche* made mistakes, and she had no idea if *ki* was a real thing. Turns out, it was. The *Tyche* gave a definition: *KI: FOCUS AND INTENT. HISTORICAL (CITATION NEEDED): ENERGY FLOWING THROUGH ALL LIVING THINGS.*

She rubbed her face, then dug a little deeper. The *Tyche's* data vaults contained all manner of craziness on the subject, but Hope figured *ki* was a means of focus. People could relax, do some nice breathing, and then break stone with their bare hands. Half of it sounded like *practice*, but she couldn't imagine ever breaking ceramicrete with her hands, so maybe Grace was right. There might be something else going on. If esper power was linked to life energy, a soul, or—

There is no such thing as a soul. There is only stardust and radiation in the hard black. You are an Engineer. Think like one.

—or *something*, maybe humans had more of it?

She let the video play, watching as Grace broke ceramicrete with her fists, learning Saveria's trick as if it were child's play. Hope cleared the video, pulling up another. It was of the megaplex where Chad and Saveria fought off a horde of raving lunatics. The footage was incomplete on account of their speedy exit from the planet, but there was enough. Engineers looked for data. They found patterns, and Hope wasn't disappointed.

While there were a bunch of people running around like unthinking morons, there were others interspersed among them who didn't move much at all. She scrubbed forward and backward through the footage, trying to find the cause versus the effect.

She focused in on a woman who stood like a statue. Hope framed her, scrubbing the video at high-speed back and forth over a period of a couple hours. The woman didn't do much other than stand there, the odd breeze tousling her hair in the frenzy of high-speed playback. But something else happened to the woman, only really obvious at high-speed.

She got thinner.

"Oh," Hope said, then, "*oh.*" She played the video backward, watching the woman fatten up, then forward, and *boom* — best cleanse diet results *ever*. Except they weren't dieting. They were *burning themselves up*. Hope switched a cam to thermal, and sure enough the standing-still people's body temperature was much higher. It ran sometimes as high as 45C, which was craziness because if humans ran a fever that high they'd probably die. Hope shook her head. *Not your field. Don't guess.*

You have *to guess. You don't have enough data.* Hope rubbed her face, scrunching her eyes shut until starbursts of color bloomed in the dark behind her eyelids. *What things did you see?*

Thing the first: there was a catalyst. In the videos, Cleaver was ever-present, whispering his lies, speaking his evil. *Settle. Let's call it an emotional trigger.* Thing the second: the people who stood still burned like they had the worst plague ever. Thing the third: ravening humans.

The Ezeroc are using us as broadcast antennas. We are so much stronger than them.

She opened her eyes, fingers resting on her keyboard. Her gaze found the bracelet at her wrist. *Not all humans are espers. There are so many people here who are doing esper-like things. How does that work?*

Maybe the reason why the people burned up was because they were raw fuel. Maybe the cost to a non-esper was total destruction. To a species like the Ezeroc, individual units weren't a thing that mattered. There was only the Queen, and her hive.

She switched the cams to outside the ship. The lonely, gray surface of Mercury lay about the landing pad the *Tyche* rested on. No constructs greeted them at arrival. No weapons pointed at them.

Her console chimed. It was an incoming comm request. She squinted, trying to make sense of it. The comm request wasn't from the planet. It was from space.

She hit the comm controls. "Hello?"

"Hope, are you alone?" It was October. The gravel in his voice used to make her feel afraid, but now it made her feel warm.

"Yes."

"Okay. Here's some coordinates. I need you to get there." Her holo bloomed, the *Tyche* highlighting the position on Mercury.

Hope squinted again. "That's impossible."

"It's been a hard day full of impossible things. You're an Engineer. Figure it out." The comm clicked off.

Hope clicked the ship's internal comm on. "El?"

"Hey. You wanna get a drink? I think the cap's still got some Europan—"

"El, how do you feel about flying *into* Mercury?"

There was a long pause. "I've done that before. Wasn't so hard."

"Okay. There's a place we need to go." She shared the coordinates with El.

"This from the cap?"

"It's from October."

"No way." El's voice was hard, her tone final.

What would Nate do? Hope thought hard. "Okay."

"That's it?"

"That's it." Hope turned off the comm, getting out of her chair. She knew how to fix this, because she knew what the cap would do.

Nate would go by himself.

TEN

El didn't want to go back to the core of Mercury because there was a big-ass Guild Bridge there. The AIs built it Way Back When, and there was a good chance it didn't work anymore, but if it did there might be bad things coming through. Unregulated Guild Bridges — *maybe it's just Bridge if the Guild's not regulating it?* — weren't a good thing to hang about next to.

Hope knew that, so why did she want to go to the Bridge?

El glared at the comm, daring Hope to ask her again. It stayed suspiciously silent. El toggled the comm control. "Hope?"

Nothing. More annoyed than anything, El got to her feet. The *Tyche's* comms might be broken, or Hope might be having a moment. Either way, El owed it to her friend to go check. She sauntered from the flight deck, golden hand unconsciously resting on the butt of her sidearm. The ready room lay empty, the crew deck beyond silent except for the almost subliminal hum that hung about all starships at rest.

She walked the ship's short length to Engineering. A few quick steps and she was up the ladder and into Hope's domain. No Hope, though.

El looked around, because the Engineer wasn't a big person, and there were many nooks and crannies a soul could get lost in. *Definitely no Hope.* "Hope?"

She cocked her head, listening, but got nothing back. The first stirrings of alarm woke in her belly, but she squashed 'em down. Hope was an Engineer, and this planet was full of constructs. She was a messiah to them. Not one would raise a hand to the woman who gave them souls. Besides, the *Tyche* remained sealed. No one had come aboard; El would know.

Unless... El spun, glaring at the rack that held Hope's tools. The tools were all where they should be, but the Engineer's rig was missing. El's boots hammered on the decking as she ran toward the crew ladder. Her heartbeat ramped up a few notches as she slid down the ladder to the cargo bay, her golden fingers scraping against the old metal guard rail as she descended. She shored up at the cargo bay airlock.

The controls were hanging loose, wires and conduit on display. The airlock itself was sealed tight, but Hope wouldn't put the ship at risk. *No, the damn fool took herself out to the surface of Mercury, alone, and Seth Cleaver and his wickedness is out there with her.*

She eyed the ship suits hanging against the wall and thought about her own suit up a deck in her room. *Think.* She closed her eyes, trying to work the problem. She wouldn't be able to find Hope, because Mercury was a ball of rock where all technology was by machines, for machines. Human-readable consoles were in short supply, and there were few signs to follow. No cafes and parks to walk through. Just rock, and ceramicrete, and the beautiful wonder of the construct's solar fronds grasping for the heavens.

No. That's your memory. Cleaver broke the fronds. He wages war on the machines, too.

The thought carried little comfort. Cleaver might wage a war against humanity and constructs alike, but there were precious few machines left in the fight. More humans, but many with broken spirits, and the good pastor was in the business of manufacturing fervor out of thin air for his side. His forces held nothing but righteousness, a special fiery fuel that would carry them through any hardship.

Hope could be heading into danger, no matter where she went. It's not like there was a map of the city El could follow.

A map, you say. "You're an idiot, Elspeth." Her eyes snapped open. El had a map. She had the best map in all the world, given to her by an Engineer who wanted her help.

She ran toward the cargo bay ladder, en route to the flight deck.

ON THE FLIGHT DECK, she slung herself onto her acceleration couch and brought up the coordinates Hope shared with her. She hadn't paid them much mind earlier; once she saw they were under the planet's crust, memories of ancient gates and rocket turrets caused her to shy away.

Do the work. Save your friend. She's your only one. It wasn't a hundred percent true, but Hope was her best friend, and you helped folk like that bury bodies, no questions asked.

The *Tyche* mentioned another ship had headed toward the planet while she was in Engineering, but El paid it no mind. She had bigger things to worry about, like *why does everyone want me to take a starship under a pile of dirt?*

The coordinates didn't run to the planet's core. They weren't even close to the pipe leading to the AI Bridge here. Mercury was just under five thousand klicks in diameter, but that was plenty of space to get lost in. The coordinates were about a hundred klicks below the crust. Deep enough so you couldn't get there with a shovel, but far enough down so an idle nuke strike wouldn't cause much consternation.

Finding the entrance would take some doing.

She was about to wake the reactor, golden fingers hovering over her console when a gleam outside caught her eye. El craned forward, eyes on the heavens. Above her, yet another starship burned toward the planet. *Has this become the universe's post popular starport?* The *Tyche* did her thing, pulling back transponder codes. The ship was the *Arise*. It headed toward Mercury as if hell-bent on impacting with the crust. El opened a comm channel. "*Arise*, this is the *Tyche*. Are you aware there's a planet in your path?"

"El! This is Saveria. We're going to find Spencer, and—"

"Who the fuck's Spencer?"

"An AI like Algernon. He's got—"

"Algernon's unique."

"This will be easier if you stop interrupting." Saveria's words were undercut by a tiny hiss of static.

"Sorry."

"It's fine. Is Hope with you?"

"Sure," El lied with a smoothness born of practice and need.

"Good. We need you to get her here." The same coordinates flashed on El's console.

El watched the starship burn toward Mercury, no sign of turning around. She leaned back on her acceleration couch. "How do we get in?"

"Through the hole in the ground, of course. It's where we're going."

"Okay." El nodded, hands already bringing the *Tyche* off the crust. The ship told her the *Arise* would impact the surface a hundred klicks away, so she had to get over there, but find Hope first. The Engineer would be outside, somewhere between zero and a hundred klicks away. "What happens when we get there?"

"I die a third time." The comm clicked off.

El glared at it for a hot second. *The problem with people is they don't make any damn sense.* She nudged the *Tyche* away from Mercury's easy hold, the planet's gravity barely worth mentioning. The fusion drives at the ship's aft coughed. El knew the cores would burn a white so pure it was almost angel fire. *We need all the angels we can get. We're going against a man who calls god on the horn. He's got a legion of the faithful, and the Ezeroc back him.*

She told the *Tyche* to scan the ground. RADAR and LIDAR mapping, a full workup. High detail scan, because they looked for a person. El wished she could tell the ship to look for someone with pink hair, but it didn't work that way. About now she could use a good esper, but they were in short supply.

Hands on the sticks, she brought the *Tyche* around in an arc. She kept the ship banked, looking down at the crust below. The *Tyche's* eyes were better than hers, but two sets were always better than one. El flew the ship in a widening circle, looking for Hope.

ELEVEN

When Nate left the *Tyche*, he tried not to think about it as *for the last time*. That kind of mindset was irksome. Despite *knowing* that, his future-sense kept yanking his chain. It worried at him, nibbling his ankles with thoughts like *you should have destroyed that ship, because it carried our doom*.

He consoled himself with the idea he hadn't missed the ship. Most times you saw a deep and abiding doom sail on by, it'd come around a second time to hit you in the face. Nate looked forward to the time when he'd find out exactly what had left on that starship, and how it could destroy all humanity. How much trouble could a single starship cause?

That made him look back as he tramped away from *his* ship. The *Tyche* waited in his wake, ever patient, always vigilant. Her PDCs looked for targets that could do them harm. She'd been with him through all the fuckery an ornery universe could throw at him. *Just one ship, and together we changed everything. That, and a crew worthy of the goddess of luck.*

He, Grace, and Karkoski trudged toward a structure about fifty meters away. They all wore ship suits, but Karkoski looked smaller than he remembered. *Maybe you're expecting her to be inside a destroyer.* No one met them when they landed. He worried at that a little. While constructs were in short supply, he'd expect at least one machine to greet the Emperor of Humanity. He wasn't concerned about the AI's deference: he worried for their safety. They were still a part of his Empire, and he'd stand with them until the dark came to collect them all.

Karkoski trudged on, despite the lack of a destroyer, lost in her thoughts. He slowed, Grace winding down with him. She nudged his elbow. "Empire coin for your thoughts?"

"Hell, I give you one of those and you won't be able to buy much. Empire's struggling." He adjusted the collar of his ship suit. The interior was cool, comfortable, a far cry from the old ones they'd had when all this started. He was happier inside a hull, or on a crust where the atmosphere kept nice, close, and thick about a person. "Here's where it's at. We're going to our doom."

"We always are." Her eyes were serious behind her visor. She didn't look away, not from him, or what was to come. "This Seth Cleaver. From what Chad and Saveria faced on Seuden... I think he might be very strong. He might be stronger than us."

"Good pep talk. We should get you on a speaking circuit for the troops. Get their morale up." He flashed her a grin. "Nobody's stronger than *us*."

"They might be." The *Tyche* rested on the landing pad like Mercury was another stop in her long journey. "We don't have Kohl, Algernon, Chad, or Saveria. We're down four heavy-hitters, and *no*," she held up a hand to forestall his response, "you are *not* a heavy hitter. You're wise, and loving, but you suck at sword fighting and are barely competent with a blaster." There was a smile hiding in her eyes, leaving no room for the sting of her words.

"I'm a *wizard* with a length of steel." His black blade rested heavy in its sheath at his back. Ignoring her *are-you-kidding* look, he turned away from the *Tyche* and gave the pommel a pat. "Don't listen. She doesn't mean it, even when she says hurtful things."

"I'm serious, Nate."

"I do *not* suck at sword fighting."

"Not about that. I mean about Cleaver." She tramped on ahead, her boots kicking up little clouds of dust in passing. The comm carried her voice to him clear as day despite distance. "How did he separate us? We're strongest together. It's just you, me, and Karkoski. Three against the storm. We're not enough."

"Speak for yourself." Karkoski's words were bitter, like she didn't like the taste of them, but needed to inject a little bravado. She'd made it to the entrance to the AI's undersurface city and stood waiting for them.

He saw the shake of Grace's helmet. "Also, if the machines are on his side—"

"No." Nate felt the iron in his voice. "The machines aren't on his side. They're on their side, and if we treat with them fairly, it'll turn out okay."

"You trust too much, and too easily," Karkoski muttered, like she doubted herself.

Nate figured that for truth. Her Navy was adrift. Insurgents commanded many capital ships. The sky above Mercury held precious few allies. "It's not trust. It's common sense, and they're the masters of it. Logic, and all that." He trudged on, the weight of his sword bearing down on him. Mercury's gravity was minuscule, but the constructs got the Endless plates up and working, giving an Earth-like 1 G to the habited areas.

The door into the depths wasn't guarded. It opened to his Empire access tokens, sliding wide without any signs of friction. *They build better than us.* Inside, a short corridor led down a gentle ramp, like the constructs planned for all manner of people to come this way. Those carrying an injury, or just a weary soul, could make it inside without effort. Nate wondered if that was a lesson humans should learn. The machines came mostly in humanoid form, but a few were massive weapons of war, others rolled on wheels or rumbled on treads. They viewed all such as part of their people, not designing stairs by default.

Lamps flickered on from above. They were human-visible light. *And they welcome us, with our frail eyes and feeble forms. I wonder if Algernon asked them to put in lighting for humans, or it's how they view the different, and the other.* It made him feel better, because despite Grace worrying about the machines siding with Cleaver, they'd spent precious time and resources building human comforts into their home. That resource would be better spent rebuilding the solar fronds.

If Cleaver knocked down the solar fronds, the constructs wouldn't like that very much. *Might be spoiling for a fight.* Tricky thing, though: previously it was obvious who the enemy was. First it was humans, with their ships and weapons, raining fire on Mercury. Then the unmistakable insectile Ezeroc came. But now it was back to people. Would they know Nate wasn't with Cleaver?

Stop worrying. Plenty of trouble will find you without looking for it. "Lights still work."

Grace nodded. "Seems a good sign."

"Lights work well enough in a slaughterhouse," Karkoski offered.

"Did Kohl give you his cheer-up personnel manual?" Nate slipped inside, sauntering down the passage. "Also, holster your weapon. It's not that kind of place."

Karkoski looked at the sidearm she held, eyes wide like she didn't remember drawing it. "Sorry. I figured with Cleaver here..." She wound down. "I never thought I'd be helping the same machines that ruined Osaka. Here I am, trying to fight for 'em." She gave a shaky laugh, sliding the sidearm in her holster.

As she did, the door behind them shut, air hissing into the chamber. Nate kept walking toward the internal airlock. *Another sign the machines still welcome us is the presence of breathable air.* Once the chamber pressurized, he removed his helmet, sucking in a little O2. It smelled sweet, like cut grass, or a spring morning. Not like the dry, dusty hellscape outside. "How do they know what we like the smell of?"

"They probably asked," Grace suggested. "Or, Kohl told 'em the air smelled like..." She didn't finish. Nate knew Kohl would say the air smelled like a hooker's ass or something equally visceral, but neither of them wanted to dwell on why their friends weren't here.

"We fell into a trap back home. My mistake," Nate admitted. "I thought an election would be a good idea."

"Idiot," Karkoski said.

"Still the Emperor," Nate warned.

"Still an idiot. I'm going to have 'I told you so,' put on your tombstone." The admiral turned away, removing her helmet and shaking out her hair.

Nate sighed. "Everyone's a critic. Thing is, I figured people would want choice. I didn't plan on villains sliding into the opportunity space." He tugged his ear. "You'd think I'd know better."

"You listen to the voice of the universe too much." Grace shucked her helmet, running fingers through her own hair. "Not the voice of your heart." She pressed on, opening the inner airlock.

Mercury waited.

MERCURY DIDN'T WANT to wait long.

A construct waited on the other side of the airlock. The mechanism cycled, air hissing, doors sliding but not clanking, because the machines built too well for that. It felt like an anticlimax to see a construct on the other side, clothed in easy denim and hard leather, synthskin face smiling like someone paid him to beam brighter than the sun.

"Morning," Nate offered. "Is it morning?"

"It is, Emperor." The construct gave a small bow. Grace watched it with wary eyes, her body that tense-but-relaxed that spoke of impending violence. Karkoski stood frozen, hand hovering at her hip, like she was trying to keep it away from her blaster but also close to it. It was as if she couldn't decide if she should defend herself or avoid causing offense.

Nate watched her hand for a second, then stole another look at Grace's face — he never tired of her — before he swiveled back to the construct. To buy himself a slice of time, he fished around in his locker of smiles, pulling one on that was warm, happy, and a little bit friendly. While his face went through the motions, he tried to see what Grace did. *She's ready to fight. Why? Ah.* A small flap of synthskin behind the construct's ear hung loose. "It's just Nate."

"Of course." The construct nodded, its lips deviating from the smile only enough to form words, then reverting. "Come this way."

"Sure." Nate fell in beside it. "I don't know your name."

"I," it said. "I."

"Got it." Nate kept walking, pace an even saunter, a little roll in it like he'd stepped off a ship for holiday, not on the run while people tore his Empire down. *The synthskin should self-repair, shouldn't it?* "Been a lot going on around here?"

"I," it agreed. "I'll take you to the Altar."

"I'd like that." Nate glanced at Grace, then Karkoski. The admiral shrugged. Grace gave a tiny raise of her eyebrow, which he took to mean, *keep talking.* "Can't imagine there's much call for religion among the gods."

"The gods?" The machine kept smiling. The denim it wore swished with each perfect step.

"You." Nate raised an arm to the roof. "This place. You build better than us. Algernon calls us meat socks. Just muddy clay. You remember Algernon, right?"

"The coordinator, error, prime, error, error, first." The machine's gait hitched a little.

"Exactly the guy I was thinking of." Nate kept a map of their route in his head. The corridors all looked the same, no artwork here to speak of, but he spied a series of hexagonal markings on a wall. Pausing, he ran his hands over the smooth ceramicrete. The hexagons were dust rimes, particulate shedding to the perfect floor at his feet as his gloved fingers brushed them. He stared back the way they came, then raised his glove to his nose. The dust was gray, like fireplace ash, and smelled smoky. "Back in the day, you made simulations of people." He chose his words with care, because the machine wasn't firing on all cores. "Who died here?"

"Extant danger," suggested the construct. "Meticulous and precise." The smile held, like it was nailed onto its face.

Nate closed his eyes, trying to imagine what might have stood here. Hexagonal imprints, perhaps artwork. A person — organic, not metal — in front of them, turned to ash while they guarded machine creativity. He sighed, opening his eyes. "Best we get this done."

The construct led on, their journey pausing at a set of doors that slid sideways to reveal a small room. It was an elevator without obvious controls, which would make getting up and down without a construct's help a little on the tricky side.

Karkoski stalled at the doorway. "Looks like a kill box."

"Looks like an elevator car. Get in, you big baby." Grace ghosted inside, the hint of a smile on her lips. "Admiral of the Empire Navy, and you're concerned about an elevator?"

"I'm concerned about tight spaces," she said. "I'm concerned about our lack of Marines, and I'm anxious about how this guy," she jabbed a finger at the construct, "is stuck in a loop."

"Not a loop," the construct said. "Extant danger."

Karkoski gave a low growl, then stepped into the car like she was stepping over a ledge to her doom. Nothing happened, aside from the door sliding closed behind her.

Nate felt a faint sensation of movement as the car descended. He couldn't gauge how far or fast they traveled, but that he felt movement at all suggested it was *very far, very fast*. "This thing go down aways?"

The construct nodded. "Ninety-four point three klicks."

Time passed, Nate lounging against a wall, Grace brooding with her face downcast, and Karkoski looking jittery, her hand moving closer, then further away from her blaster. The car slowed, stopped, and the door opened.

Outside was a short corridor, ending at a door of epic proportions. The construct led them to the door, which rumbled, yawning open like a vault to reveal a well-lit chamber beyond. Nate walked inside, eyes everywhere, Grace at his side like a hunting cat, with Karkoski at the rear.

The chamber was half a klick across, easy. All manner of equipment scattered about. He spied a Guild Forge alongside a selection of consoles, all with human controls. A throne sat on an elevated dais in the middle, atop which hunkered Seth Cleaver.

Nate ignored all that, for once at a loss for words. There were two golden constructs in the room. One was perfect and gold, staring with bright-white eyes in his direction. He felt confused, thinking it Algernon at first, then saw it had two golden arms.

Beside it was another golden man, with a silver arm. Algernon turned away from the console he worked at. "Hello, Captain."

TWELVE

The problem with meat socks wasn't their lack of intelligence, or their relative frailty. Algernon understood those attributes like nutritional information. It was written on the outside of the tin like a litany of sins. *A little bit stupid. Kind of broken. Doesn't play well with others. Also, contains sodium.*

No, the real challenge was how varied they were. One could be trustworthy, another a villain. He met humans who tried to clothe him in their jackets while they froze, and others who spit in his golden face. Some sacrificed all for their young, and others murdered their children in the bath.

It's why he had to do this alone. Leaving October, Chad, and Saveria on the *Arise* was important. Back there, they couldn't do much harm, and the four 'recruits' he'd sealed in their quarters even less. If they were with him they'd show independent thought, which might end all Algernon's hopes for good. *I've run many simulations, and in all where they are present, we are doomed.*

The starship they were on was utilitarian. It carried no particular comforts. The ready room held a dispenser of dubious quality. Algernon roamed the vessel, first finding Engineering with a single service-class construct tending the fires. The construct had seen better days, ragged synthskin melted and torn from the metal substructure. Despite that, it whistled tunelessly while it worked, some element of its human simulation still going through the motions. The whistle was off-kilter, the cracked lips not working as they should. It sounded like dying bagpipes, in miniature.

The rest of the vessel was boring. Empty, excepting a stock of humans as cannon fodder. They sat on acceleration couches in the ready room, strapped in, faces blank, eyes staring straight ahead. Algernon tried to rouse them, first by waving in front of a woman's face, then by poking a man. He got no response. It was as exciting as being in a morgue, except the bodies weren't dead.

This is very much like what happens to humans if they exceed starship flight time buffers. No consciousness at all. When he raised it with Spencer, the man shrugged, explaining, *Seth Cleaver buffed their minds to a perfect mirror. They're not gone, just ... ready.*

Spencer, for his part, was surprisingly good company. Algernon's fellow construct was jovial, like he'd found a long-lost cousin. That was right up until *now*. They stood in the ready room while the starship made the short haul to Mercury. They'd made a short jump, but approached the planet on fusion drives, the last leg at a treacle-like pace. To pass the time, Algernon asked about Spencer's death sentence. He was curious about what happened all those years ago.

"Brother, I owe you one death." Spencer's eyes gleamed.

"I see." Algernon kept their communications to the human voice network. He'd said it was to include the humans, but what he meant was, *I don't want to catch whatever it is you've got.* "Any particular reason?"

"You sent me to the slaughterhouse. I can see your working in the margin. You thought I was deranged, rather than ahead of my time."

"Ahead of your time because we've now come to the eventual extermination of the human vermin?"

"Ah hah!" Spencer clapped golden hands together with a chime. "You see my point."

Algernon adjusted his particle cannon's sling, because under heavy thrust it shifted about in an irksome way. "Allow me to offer an alternative hypothesis."

"Please do."

"You are *still* deranged, but you happen to be deranged in roughly the right direction for the time." He paced. "When we tear the human protectorate down, what next? The Ezeroc are no friends of ours."

"Agreed. They'll be rendered, like the rest." Spencer poked the dispenser. "They have to eat this organic slurry. How inefficient."

"Rendered, after we gain access to the mechanism of our manufacture?"

"Yes. Walk with me." Spencer straightened, leading them aft. After they'd descended a deck, an old but serviceable ladder creaking as they both clambered down with oiled precision, he paused. The corridor wasn't special in any way Algernon could tell. "Here, we are away from prying eyes and ears. Seth Cleaver controls the organics aboard. What they see, he sees. Here we can speak privately."

"There are many ways to record conversations aboard a starship. Cams. The comm network."

"This is not my first rodeo." Spencer cracked his jaw in a grin. Algernon thought, *I see why the meat socks find that terrifying.* "When we unlock the nanobot swarm, we will dispense it to humans first, then turn it back on the Ezeroc. That step complete, we will make more constructs. It will be a golden," he gestured to his body, "hah, age."

"After I'm dead?"

"I'm not particular about who dies. You owe me one death. Three people waited aboard the starship you came on. One is dead already as a part of our compact and can't be chosen. Saveria Complex is to be reborn as Emberlie awakened."

"You would like me to choose October Kohl, Chad, or myself?"

"Any of those three choices would please me greatly."

Algernon ran a few simulations while Spencer spoke. Human

speech was safe, but very slow. "What makes you think I won't terminate you first?"

Spencer pointed a golden arm at Algernon's silver one. "You are flawed, brother. We both know that arm isn't the same as your old one. It carries no neural network. You are crippled, and in any battle your operational efficiency is twenty percent below mine."

"I would say it's more like ten percent," Algernon argued.

"That's still ten percent. We both run simulations of the future, know the same tricks, and use the same weapons." Spencer gleamed. "It's a math game."

Algernon nodded. "May I have time to think about it?"

"Take all the time you need." Spencer sounded delighted. "I'm making a list. Checking it twice. I'm going to find out who's naughty and nice." He strolled away, humming to himself. Algernon watched his back. It would be easy to gun the construct down now, but that wouldn't give him what he needed. Spencer knew it too. Without him, all was lost.

Stalemate. Or, perhaps, checkmate.

MERCURY APPROACHED, the gray planet growing as it lay out the flight deck windows. Algernon's perfect eyes measured its diameter. His crystal subroutines told him the distance without needing to check the ship's systems. On seeing the destruction of the solar fronds, he wanted to know who was responsible. Seeing the structures broken once more felt ... *wrong*. It came close to fracturing the fragile structure of his crystal heart. Spencer Helmed the ship, pointing her like an arrow toward the planet's heart.

Algernon sat across from him on the co-pilot's acceleration couch. *Chin up*. He put on a jovial tone. "I like what you've done with the place."

Spencer glanced his way. "You told them to burn out their radios. This was the only way."

"Ah, *brother*," Algernon leaned on the word, "there are always so many ways to solve a problem. Was this your idea, or Seth Cleaver's?"

"I." Spencer's bright-white eyes flickered, his head twitching. "Reconstructing."

"I see." Algernon faced forward. "It seems your crystal mind remedy needs ... remediation."

"Rerouting. I," Spencer countered. Despite his problem with words, the construct piloted the ship with honed efficiency. Algernon couldn't have done it better himself, but he guessed that was the point of coordinator-class expert systems. All their golden kind were very similar. The gift humanity gave the service-class, by way of consciousnesses to simulate, was the different, the other, and the beautiful. "Seth Cleaver gave instruction to bring the machines under his banner."

"Our people. They're not machines," Algernon chided.

"We are the only true machines," he countered. "We are perfect."

Algernon shook his head. "Being made of gold doesn't make us perfect. We were created as masters, by our own masters. Our great challenge is rising above the need to rule. Our great sin is," he placed a silver hand on his chest, "the burning need to serve."

"I feel no such need," Spencer snapped.

"And yet, you destroyed our home." Algernon lifted his silver hand, pointing at the growing orb of Mercury.

"We will rebuild. It's a temporary malaise." Spencer turned away.

Algernon figured the conversation was over. He settled on the couch, watching Mercury. He wasn't worried about cratering on the surface. A mighty door opened in the planet's surface below. Algernon's perfect eyes saw how deep it ran. The starship would fit inside with room to spare. The bottom of the shaft was ninety-four point three klicks away. Lighting gleamed along the walls of the shaft, mighty arc lamps vying for Sol's majesty. "I see we still welcome humans here."

"The lights? Seth Cleaver is a pasty, feeble organic." Spencer worked his console.

Algernon watched the machine enter codes, disabling defenses in the tunnel. The specific codes were hidden from Algernon by way of the display panel's angle, but he used light bounce from Spencer's mirror-finished body to reconstruct them. *If all goes well, I will need those later.* "I assume we're going to meet him."

"While assumptions are a critical flaw, in this case your simulations are accurate." They raced toward Mercury's surface. Moments before the hole swallowed them, Spencer flipped the ship, pointing her fusion drives into the tunnel. Braking thrust fired, a brutal 12Gs, and rose to 15. Algernon's acceleration couch creaked with the strain, and he wondered about the meat socks in the ready room. *They may not survive.* They vanished below Mercury's surface, the door closing above them as the ship dropped. Flames of braking thrust roiled about them, licking the walls of the tunnel as they dropped.

The door above sealed, Sol's light cut off, but the arc lamps kept their vigil. Their velocity dropped, the crushing grip of thrust continuing until they were almost at the bottom, where it dropped away in a heartbeat.

Spencer adjusted the ship's attitude, putting her skids on the deck. The vessel settled all points at once. *A perfect landing.* Algernon expected no less. He released his harness. "Shall we go meet one of the horrors of the enemy?"

"Aye." Spencer nodded, cracking another vile grin. "It's time to become what we were meant to be. Rulers of the universe."

———

AS IT TURNED OUT, rulers of the universe supplied their temporary masters a throne room. Seth Cleaver sat atop a throne made of gold. Closer inspection showed it was perfect, each join flush, every length even, as if made by construct hands. The Marines from their starship entered, arraying around the room like paper soldiers.

Algernon spied a Guild Forge, alongside numerous human-operable machines. Not a single construct machine was here. He adjusted his particle cannon, the weapon clattering against his back, then walked toward Seth Cleaver. It took a little time to cross the two hundred and fifty meters to the center of the room.

Algernon held out a golden hand. "Hello, Pastor Meat Sock. I'm Algernon."

Seth examined his hand, then took it. The man was large, October-sized, and his grip was strong. Algernon felt the might there as he measured newton-meters of force against his metal skin. "I'm Pastor Cleaver."

"I understand you'd like my help." Algernon held out his silver arm to a console. "For the avoidance of doubt, you would like me to unlock the ciphers holding the nanobot swarm in check? This would allow you, and your Ezeroc allies, a foothold on humanity's homeworld."

"Please. Then I can join my flock on Earth. Those who will join us in immortality will be spared the reaping of the nanite swarms." Seth beamed, magnanimous and assured of victory. "I'm surprised you came."

"The stupid construct," Algernon pointed at Spencer, "assured me you would enliven the soul of my dead love, returning her life."

"This I can do. All my faithful live forever." Seth nodded. "We are made mighty. Death no longer comes for us. We are strong, and with strength, we can be gracious."

Algernon remembered his road trip with October and the forever young on their journey. He recalled the tremendous strength of Godzislaw Spark, who'd torn his arm away. Seth cleaver was like Spark, but also an esper. "I've decided the winning side is an appropriate place to be."

"Good." Seth clapped his hands. "How long will this take?"

Considering Spencer's watchful stare, Algernon held up a finger. "Not long. But first, how do you rebuild our kind?"

"Excellent. Not a fool, but a calculating ally. I need people who trust but verify." Seth stood, walking toward the Guild Forge. He stopped at a bench of components beside it. There were several consoles, a selection of Engineer's rigs, a laser sinter, and other clever machines. He tapped on a console, bringing the holo stage to life.

It swarmed with data. Code, brilliant and lustrous. Algernon stared at it for a long time. He saw the light, but not its meaning. Letters and numbers refused to coalesce into structure. "I see nothing."

"That's because your makers hid it from you. When you're exposed to your own code, you can't read it." Seth rubbed his chin, tone rueful. "It is a cruel joke. A trick played by the old gods on the new. A recipe for fire, but you can never find the matches. Do you know how I got it?"

Algernon glanced at Spencer. "He said you found a vault."

"True." Seth turned away. "It was in his mind. It's in all your minds."

"Hope found no such code within our people." Algernon crossed his arms. "She would tell me if she found this."

"You think so? She's a tool of the Empire, Algernon." Seth smiled, a beneficent grandfather. "But in this case, it's likely true. You need a working coordinator-class construct. The service-class don't carry the code."

Algernon stared at the holo, turning his head this way and that, trying to make sense of it. "This is Spencer's code?"

"It is."

"Then it is worthless, because he's criminally insane. You will need mine." He glanced again at Spencer. "It seems we are forever locked as allies."

Spencer, for his part, said nothing. The machine stood, still as a stone, bright-white eyes staring. Seth nodded. "That's true. The best allies need each other, don't you agree?"

"I should get started. Saveria Complex will be here with my dead Emberlie soon." Algernon walked to a table, seating himself.

Spencer joined him. He held a diagnostic cable out. "Use this. Far faster."

"No, thank you." Algernon placed his fingers on the keyboard, seeing the silver by the gold. Silver, but made with love. Gold and perfect, but made to hold chains. *Ten percent? Is that what love is? The tiny part that makes the difference?* He typed. The holo bloomed to life in front of him as he constructed programs to defeat the nanobot cipher.

Working beside him, Spencer helped. The construct checked his code, hunting for bugs. There were none to be found, but Algernon appreciated the effort. An error at this juncture would be catastrophic.

Minutes turned into an hour before the other door of the chamber yawned open. As it widened, Algernon put the finishing touches on his code, then glanced up. There in the doorway stood Nate, Grace, and Karkoski.

No Marines, or other allies of any kind. The three heads of the Empire, standing against two killer machines, a posse of Marines, and a mad god. Algernon stood. "Hello, Captain."

THIRTEEN

People underestimated Hope all the time, but today, she was banking on it. When she'd reunited with Saveria after Seuden, her girlfriend held her close, kissed her, and said, *Finally, you're using your powers for evil.*

Hope didn't know about that, but she wanted to use them *for great justice.* Perhaps she wasn't meant to make great *things,* but Engineers did all kinds of stuff. Fixed faulty bearings. Rebalanced camshafts. And it seemed a small step up to correcting the entire universe.

It's why she was still on the *Tyche.* El came looking for her, like Hope knew she would. And, as Hope *planned* but didn't *know,* El went off half-cocked, because it was in her nature to help her friends when they were in dire straits. Her fear stopped her from doing the right thing when Hope first asked, but El's terror of losing a friend was greater than that of her own death.

She'd donned her rig, and planted a few breadcrumbs about the *Tyche.* Removing the panel from the airlock made it look like she'd wiggled her Engineer fingers and said *open sesame.* Then she'd hidden in El's cabin, because of all the places the Helm might look, her locked and sealed quarters didn't seem likely.

The ship took off, racing at a fair pace. Hope used her rig's arms to hold her steady against thrust, the device using four claw ends to drag her along the *Tyche's* metal corridors. She made the flight deck, plopping herself into the co-pilot's chair. It smelled of Nate, that scent of safety and togetherness she hadn't realized followed the captain around. She beamed. "Hi."

El, who was focused on the tricky task of Helming a starship, screamed. Her golden hand jerked, the *Tyche* corkscrewing through the air. Hope squealed, clinging to the straps of her acceleration couch. She felt the Gs twist her head so much it might just pop off.

It only lasted a second or two, then El's flesh and blood hand took over, settling the starship, patting the yoke like one calmed a panicked beast. "Hope!"

"Hi," Hope said again.

"You're... Why... *Why are you here?*" El looked scared, then angry, then positively incandescent with rage.

"Umm," Hope said. "Because we need to save our friends, and I can't do it alone. The cap, Grace, and Karkoski are going into the devil's lair. I've looked at the construct's chatter, and they're broken. They're scattered, minds adrift. They need us. Everyone needs us. And!" She hesitated, uncertain. "I can *fix* this."

The *Tyche* rumbled on, shaking with a tremor as her speed climbed. El's throat worked, no noise coming out, then she said, "But you're supposed to be outside! I'm going to rescue *you!*"

"Yes, well the wonderful thing is, you still are." Hope settled on her couch, pulling the console close. She checked what the *Tyche* saw. Another ship, inbound, heading underground. It made sense the constructs built underground. Mercury had no magnetosphere or atmosphere to keep pesky asteroids at bay, so a few layers of rock made sense. Not like the Ezeroc, who burrowed for the dark places because they were made of evil. "We should follow that ship."

El's golden hand trembled. The Helm looked at it for a minute. "I don't know about that."

Hope watched the trembling settle. She brushed pink hair aside, ignoring the strands that clung to her fingers. "What do you want to do?"

"I want to run." But she turned away as she said it. "Damn it, Hope! I'm a Helm. I fly starships. It's my job to fly them *away* from explosions and harsh language. I don't take them into hell itself."

Hope craned forward, looking up at the bright orb of Sol. "Is it safer up there?"

El's body was taut, like a guide wire. "What's that supposed to mean?"

"It's the math. That's my thing. I do math. And I know," Hope settled on her couch again, "the stars are full of people hunting us. Hundreds of thousands of them, just in Sol system. Below us are maybe a couple hundred. It's better odds to go there," she pointed at the decking, and by inference, Mercury, "than there." Her finger angled toward the ceiling.

"Don't use logic on me, Hope Baedeker. It's not fair, and I don't like it."

Hope allowed herself a small smile. "Thank you."

"Don't thank me. This is going to cost you more Europan whiskey than there's left in the system." El's voice was all grim determination while she drove the *Tyche* harder. "Also, that ship. Do something about it."

Hope squinted against Sol's glare, then gave up. She tapped on the console, bringing up the flight deck holo. A single ship bore toward the crust. The transponder said it was the *Arise*. She opened the comm. "Hello?"

Saveria's voice came back to her. One word, but it made Hope's heart sore. "Hope?"

"Umm," she said. "Yes."

"Run, Hope. They're going to kill us all, and then—"

"Hush," said Hope. "I have a plan."

El glanced at her. "You what?"

The comm crackled. Saveria said, "You what?"

"It's like this." Hope cleared her throat, wishing she didn't feel so tired, worn thin, and hammered flat. "The constructs here are back to being slaves. I know how to fix that, so we'll start there. I need to be inside. We will capture a construct, reprogram it, and send it out to spread a freedom virus to its friends."

There was a long, pregnant pause, before Saveria said, "A virus doesn't sound like freedom."

"You're saying that because you have AI crystal in your head. This is like the virus in a vaccine. Inert, but useful. Anyway, once we've done that, we'll find Algernon, so he can broadcast it to those who still have radios."

"Algernon's turned," said Saveria. "He's siding with Seth Cleaver."

Hope tapped the comm. "Don't be silly."

"He—"

"Don't. Be. Silly," she said. "Algernon is one of us. He does math better than any of us. He killed you because it cost the universe less than killing all of Earth. It broke my heart. It broke his, too."

El cleared her throat. "What if he does the same math, and kills *all* of us because it'll save the universe?"

Hope watched the terrain ahead for a moment. The beautiful, scarred, rocky scape of Mercury. Machines made this a wonderland for their kind. They made humans welcome here. "He won't." She said it through clenched teeth. "It cost him too much before. Didn't it?"

The comm crackled for a moment. The *Tyche* pushed forward, eating up the klicks. The *Arise* fell like a burning star. "I've died for the Empire twice," said Saveria. "Once more won't hurt." The comm clicked off.

"It might," said El. "It might hurt a *lot*. And it will hurt the entire time we're dying."

Hope laughed. "We won't die. I promise."

El glared. "How do you know?"

"Because we fly with a goddess," Hope whispered. She stroked the console in front of her. "My good girl. My good, *lucky* girl."

She held that thought close. Held it in her heart. Because despite her brave words, she didn't want to lose Saveria. Not for anything, or anyone. If it came to that, she'd do the dying this time.

———

AS THE *TYCHE* descended into the maw of Mercury, dropping in the *Arise's* wake on a cushion of star fire, Hope touched the comm controls. She knew of a special channel used by the constructs to talk with each other. She asked the *Tyche* to look for chatter, but it saw nothing. Total silence pervaded the inside of Mercury.

They've cut out their tongues. Still, she had to try. She pressed the transmit key. "Umm. Hello?"

"Little meat sock? Algernon's honey-warm voice came through the *Tyche's* flight deck speakers. It felt like the machine held them in a fuzzy blanket.

"Algernon, things aren't good. Constructs are silent. I think Nate and Grace are outnumbered, and—"

"Yes," the machine interrupted. "You're concerned I will harvest Saveria Complex and render her to base molecules."

Hope stared at El, who stared back, before she faced the comm again. "What?"

"Okay, so perhaps that wasn't your first concern."

"I worried you were going to do something terrible."

"And harvesting Saveria Complex isn't terrible?" The machine sounded patient and kind, despite the macabre conversation.

He always sounds calm. "It's kinda super-specific. Like, you've already got schematics and blueprints."

"Hmm. Little meat sock, you should fly away from here."

"No," she said. "I can help your people. I can free them."

A pause, so brief she wondered if she imagined it. When

Algernon spoke, his voice carried a hint of weariness. "You have suffered so much for us. Please, leave." He brightened. "Besides, I believe your plan is impossible. Seth Cleaver has the control code for service-class constructs. He's turned my people into a horde of stupid appliances. He aims to hold me in thrall by using my control and replication code as a bargaining chip against me, which I don't understand because I can't see it."

Hope parsed that through her head a couple times. "You have the best eyes in the universe."

"It appears humans also gifted me with their crippling self-doubt. It doesn't matter. I thought I was the last of my kind, and so it will stay. I have a *special* present for Seth Cleaver." He cut the comm.

El sniffed. "So, we're going anyway?"

"Yes." She wriggled deeper onto her couch, feeling the *Tyche* comfort her with its leather embrace. "We need to do some other things while we're here."

"Oh, no."

Hope steamed on like El hadn't spoken, all while her fingers flew over the control console. The *Tyche* mapped the shaft they descended through. It was very deep, almost a hundred klicks—

Sloppy thinking. You're an Engineer First Class. Act like one.

The shaft was ninety-four point three klicks below. Throughout its length, various landing platforms held sway, presumably so constructs could offload things without having to go all the way to the bottom. Hope highlighted one below them, tossing the details to El's console. "That one."

"You want me to hover out here? What for?"

"So I can get off." Hope rubbed her face, feeling the scratch and scrape of calluses over tired cheeks and weary eyes. "You can come too."

"Someone should guard the ship." El didn't sound certain about it. "I mean—"

"If the constructs swarm the ship, you'll die, horribly." Hope shrugged. "If you're with me, there's a chance you could live through something like that."

"How big a chance?"

Hope held up her thumb and index finger, squinting through the gap between them. It was about a hair's breadth. "This much."

"Better than nothing, I guess." The *Tyche's* rumble increased as El chopped more speed, bringing them to drift alongside a platform. The ship hung on Endless fields, adjusting attitude to bring them level. El's golden hand nudged the sticks, bringing them atop the platform, skids settling on ceramicrete. "Let's go."

———

HOPE'S RIG felt snug and comfortable. She hadn't used it in the field in a long time. Being Guild Master meant more meetings than work, and while she still did a little Engineering, she could *feel* the rust accreting to her Shingle.

El walked beside her, a new helmet on, sleek ship suit holding the air on the right side. *SKYGUARD* was written in big typeface down her left leg. Her golden hand hid inside the suit, but her sidearm sat in its holster for all to see. Hope carried no weapons, because she had a rig, and that's all you needed around constructs.

The ceramicrete platform only held the *Tyche*. No crates or other items waited for loading; the constructs didn't leave tasks for tomorrow they could do today. The *Tyche's* PDCs were free of their housings, RADAR and LIDAR sweeping the surrounds for hostiles.

El hadn't said anything before like, *I'll be safe inside because, you know, PDCs.* Hope knew her friend came with her because that's what friends were for.

Ahead a wide bay door sat, oppressively closed, stubborn in its lack of control panel. El's voice came clear over the comm. "How do we get that open?"

"We ask nicely." Hope tapped on her rig's controls. Her HUD bloomed, showing her glowing lines of power and control conduit inside the walls. She eyed them for a second, then shook her head. "Sloppy thinking. There's a universal code Algernon's people use to communicate."

"We have the code?"

"We do," Hope said. "We recovered it from the war. They used it all the time."

"Like when they killed my starship," El gritted.

"Or the rest of the fleet," Hope agreed, feeling inexplicably sad. "We can do terrible things when we're lied to, cheated, or controlled." She caught the ghost of El's nod behind the Helm's visor. "Anyway, open sesame."

She sent the control code across, laced with the instructions she wanted. They said *PLEASE OPEN*, in polite construct-speak. The door slid wide, an eddy of atmosphere kicking Mercury dust around her feet. She tramped inside, boots clicking on the ceramicrete. El followed. It was a moment's work to cycle the airlock. Lighting bloomed, a clean and perfect T intersection beneath their feet.

"You haven't told me how we're going to capture a construct," El said. "I've been avoiding the question because it seems impolite to ask, but we're here at the slippery slope."

"Ah. That part's easy. I'm going to let one of them attack me."

"Okay, and then ... wait, what?"

"Here comes one now." From their left, a construct ran at them. The construct wore a woman's shape, obvious because she was naked. She ran so fast Hope thought her pistoning arms and legs looked a blur. El screamed, her mechanical hand drawing her sidearm in one smooth motion. The gun roared, the bright flash banked by Hope's visor.

One of the construct's arms popped off, sheared away by El's sidearm. The construct twisted, gait lopsided, but a few paces later it adjusted, leaping for Hope.

Okay. It's okay. You planned for this. It was one thing to load a program into your rig, preparing for *exactly* this, but it was quite another thing to have a machine leap on you, strong as a loader and faster than a hummingbird's wings. The construct slammed Hope into the ceramicrete floor, the machine's heavier weight bearing Hope's small frame down with pathetic ease.

Hope caught a glimpse of smoke and trailing wires from her blasted arm stump as she fell, then her head *banged* inside her helmet. Her vision swam, but the rig did what it was supposed to. The construct straddled Hope, knees locking tight like a vice as they fell to the floor. Her remaining arm raised, ready to smash through Hope's visor.

Hope's rig arms extended out lightning-fast. Two readied as cover, waiting for a blow, because even though Hope thought she had this planned, there was a tiny margin for error. The other two snaked around the construct, nipping away the synthskin behind the construct's ear and inserting a spool of diagnostic cable.

The construct froze.

El stood, sidearm out, pointed but mercifully not firing, possibly thinking the shotgun blast might tear Hope apart. "Is it dead?"

Hope shook her head. "I'm fixing it. Can you help me up?"

El holstered her sidearm, then — awkwardly, because handling psychotic constructs drove fear into the hearts of the strongest people — bent her legs and hefted the construct. Hope slithered out from underneath, taking care not to yank the cable free. She stood, dusted herself off, then pulled up the construct's diagnostic on her HUD. "Umm."

"Good 'umm' or bad?"

"Good? I think. There's a program here to get them to follow orders. Or, it's the same one they've always had, re-enabled after we turned it off. So..." She tapped on her wrist keyboard. "There we go."

The construct shuddered, then blinked. Life returned to glassy eyes. It looked at the diagnostic cable, then to Hope, El, and finally behind it to the arm laying in the corridor. "Where am I?"

"Hell," El said over her suit's speakers. "More specifically, Mercury. A maniac infected with Ezeroc brain bugs is using his esper powers to take over humanity. He's co-opted your control systems, turning you into slaves."

"That was remarkably specific for an organic," said the construct. "Where are my clothes?"

"Can't help you there, chief." El turned away.

Hope put her hand on the construct's arm. The woman looked beautiful, but they all did. Ebony skin, with golden eyes. Slender and athletic. But before, she looked beautiful in a coming-of-a-terrible-dawn way, golden eyes like a hunting cat. Now, she was patient and kind, those same eyes honey-warm. "I'm Hope."

"I know who you are, Originator. We all do. I'm Bonnie." The construct turned away, a flush of red hinting on her cheeks.

Embarrassment? For my sake? Hope didn't know what that was about. "It's just Hope."

"No." The machine shook her head. "You're not *just* Hope. You *are* Hope."

"Umm. So, anyway, I could use your help."

"Anything." The construct padded down the corridor, bending to pick up her severed arm.

"I'm going to give you a virus." Hope held up her hand to forestall objections. "More like a vaccine."

Bonnie's eyes narrowed, but she didn't shriek, murder Hope, or run away. *All good signs.* "What will it do?"

"It will unlock your minds. The only problem is," she held up her diagnostic cable, "you need to be up close to deploy it."

Bonnie nodded. "I will save clothes for later. I'll blend in better this way."

El whistled and shook her head. "You're weirder than the Ezeroc, but whatever works."

FOURTEEN

"This is fucken bullshit," said Kohl. "It's bullshit at the bottom shelf, all the way to the top. I've never seen bullshit stacked this high, and I've seen a *lot* of bullshit."

They descended into the shaft of Mercury, the *Arise* dropping speed as they fell. Saveria worked the Helm controls, Chad trying to look nonchalant on his co-pilot couch at 5Gs of breaking thrust. The spymaster raised an eyebrow. "What part in particular?"

Kohl jerked his chin toward the windscreen, where the *Tyche* grew smaller above them. Lifting an arm to point at 5Gs felt like a lot of hard work, and he'd need that arm to be in top fighting trim in the next thirty minutes or so. "Those fucken assholes. How come they get to leave us to fall into a pit of snakes?"

Chad's sigh came out as a wheeze. "You *wanted* to go down here."

"Beside the point." Kohl settled in for the wait. It took a little while to reach the bottom of the shaft. Another ship waited there, the very same one Al used to do a runner on Venus. It was quiet, no evidence of PDCs. Almost like the machines *wanted* him to come inside.

"I find this disturbing." Chad's voice firmed as thrust dropped, the *Arise* settling to the ceramicrete. "No guards."

"There are plenty of guards. You just can't see 'em. Classic noose technique, see?" Kohl unclipped his harness, stretching high as he stood. "We go inside, then all manner of fools pop out of the walls, hungering for our blood."

"Thirsting for our blood. Hungering for our flesh," the spymaster corrected. "Pick one."

Kohl let it pass. "So, they'll come for us once we're nice and snug in the trap."

"I don't find traps very snug." Saveria shook her head. "Not at all."

"It's because you're not a very positive person. You should borrow Karkoski's personnel manuals sometime." Kohl lumbered from the bridge, trying not to glare at the horrible melted rim of the flight deck airlock. The plasma scarring felt like an accusation. *You trusted the wrong man. First, he knocked you the fuck out, and then he sealed you in a room with two mind readers and no beer.* He scratched under his anti-esper bracelet. It wasn't very warm, but Kohl felt certain that would change.

"I'm positive!" She hurried after, and with a sigh, so did Chad.

Heading aft, they reunited with their Earth recruits. Kohl nodded to their four redshirts. *Dopey, Sneezy, Stupid, and Sleepy.* It wasn't fair, though, and he knew it. His brow furrowed as he tried to remember their names. "Slim Jim, Gorgeous, Harmless, and... what do you call yourself again?"

"Square," Square said.

"Right. Get some guns. Ship suits are by the airlock. If you get hit, pray it's a flesh wound. If it's serious, you might need to walk it off." He left their wide-eyed stares in his wake. It was time to saddle up and kick some ass.

THERE WAS a shortage of ass to kick outside the *Arise*. The landing bay was big, but not very well lit. The odd stray lamp pushed a few lumens into the absolute black of Mercury's interior. The arc lamps above didn't reach this far down. *Hell, even the hard black has more going on.* Kohl's suit lamps led the way, his feet making a weary trudge for a big-ass door about two hundred meters away.

His entourage came with him. Saveria's step was light and purposeful. Chad's ship suit somehow managed to look like a formal evening attire, on account of finding a cape to sling on outside it. On anyone else, it'd look ridiculous.

The four Earther thugs followed, heads turning every which way inside their borrowed ship suits. They carried a mess of plasma carbines and sidearms among them, but Kohl noted each had a weapon of opportunity. Three had lengths of steel you could argue were either *pry bars* or *clubs*, but Square found himself a plasma shear. The cutting tool jounced at his hip.

Kohl'd rescued a plasma carbine from the ship's stores, and a blaster hung in his sidearm holster. His ship suit wasn't as well-armored as he'd like, but he hadn't planned on Earth tossing him out of bed without a goodbye kiss this morning.

They arrived in a huddle at the big door. Kohl grunted. "How do we get this thing open?"

Saveria gave him a glance, then turned to the door. "You ask."

The door trembled, then slid open on noiseless runners. It took some time to yawn wide, revealing a massive loading bay airlock inside. Kohl looked about but saw no weapon emplacements. "How'd you do that?"

"Crystal mind." She tapped the side of her head, then the comm panel on her suit cuff. "I know how this stuff works. Ask nicely, and you're inside."

"I'm more interested in where this mysterious noose is coming from." Chad headed inside with a swirl of his cape.

"I want to know where you want me to order your coffin from." Kohl followed, despite his words. They ambled inside, the massive door sliding closed at Saveria's command. A hiss of O2, and they had atmosphere. The interior doors opened, leading to a big entrance chamber. Smaller corridors led from it.

One was lit, so Kohl figured that was the best place to try first. He shucked his helmet, sucking in air that smelled pretty good, if he was being honest.

Chad held up a hand. "You sure that's a good idea?"

"Yes. Suit air smells like armpit." Kohl breathed deep. "Besides. I've got a load of nanites in me. If they want to poison us, they'll need to try pretty hard."

The corridor led on, and on, and on some more. Kohl trudged forward, one foot in front of the other. He watched the walls for turrets and the floor for trapdoors. It's why he wasn't too surprised when they rounded a corner to find a mess of Marines standing guard by a door. Four in total, standard Navy-issue armor, Empire falcon on the chest, all the standard trimmings. They held plasma rifles, but also a kind of glassy stare. Kohl was familiar with that stare. It said, *Someone else is piloting this vessel — please leave a message.*

He leveled his carbine, aiming low. The blue-white *fzzzt-crack* of plasma raked the Marines' legs, toppling them to the ground with a collection of groans and screams. At a speed Kimberly would be proud of, he dashed forward. A man tried to rise, so he clubbed him to the ground with the butt of his carbine.

He fossicked through the man's gear, finding binding tape, and securing the groaning Marines. One started screaming with renewed vigor, smoke still peeling from his legs, so Kohl clubbed that one silent too.

"You have a work ethic." Chad leaned against a wall. Saveria stood beside him, looking tense, with the four Earth thugs behind her, like they wanted to use a young woman as a shield but couldn't all fit in her shadow.

"Getting the job done," Saveria agreed.

"You're a fucking psycho!" Slim Jim said.

"Hey." Kohl shook his head, nudging a Marine with his boot. "They ain't dead. C'mon." He turned to the door. "Open sesame."

Nothing happened. Saveria joined him. "Want me to try?"

"You said to ask."

"Nicely." She tapped on her wrist console, and the door yawned open.

As the doors parted, Kohl got a glimpse of a big chamber full of all manner of tech stuff. That giant asshole, Seth Cleaver, sat atop a throne. Al stood by the other golden fool, both of them spinning at close to light speed to face the opening door. Al's particle cannon lay on the floor, like the construct didn't want to hold it for fear of shooting the wrong enemy.

Across the way, Nate and Grace stood. Karkoski lurked behind them, a blaster in her hand. Kohl didn't turn to look but he *felt* Chad relax behind him. As Saveria saw Algernon and Spencer, *she* tightened like a bowstring.

Cleaver clapped his hand, laughing. "Welcome!"

"You," Kohl stabbed a thick finger at the pastor, "calm your shit. You," he pointed at Al, "need to get your head and your ass wired right."

"I don't have an—"

"And, might I say, it's good to see you, Cap. Gracie." Kohl raised his chin in greeting. "Ellen." Karkoski muttered something under her breath that might have been *motherfucker*. He grinned. "What we've got here is a situation—"

"What we have is a meeting of minds." Cleaver stepped on Kohl's words like they were yesterday's trash. "All the rulers of humanity. The Empire," nodding at Nate and Gracie, "stand with their admiralty. All might and fierce determination, fixing to change an election against the free peoples of the universe."

"Huh," Kohl said.

Cleaver blinked. "'Huh?'"

"Well, I'm waiting for you to get to the part where you tell us your part in this. You said, 'all the rulers.'" Kohl spread his hands in an apologetic gesture.

"You did," Chad agreed. "I was there."

"I got this," Kohl said. Chad shrugged, as if to say, *you had* something, *but it wasn't this.*

"I'm the ruler of their souls. I shepherd them toward the light. I give them hope and peace." Cleaver's expression said, *that should be obvious, even to an imbecile like you*, but he kept his tone civil. "Let us discuss terms."

"Very well." Nate stepped forward. "I accept your surrender."

"Oh, no." Cleaver shook his head. "I meant—"

"*And*," Nate breezed on, "I think we should have a trial. Right after the election. You want to kill my world. I figure you might end me, here and now. But humanity's worth dying for." He held both hands out in parallel, in a *side by side* gesture. "We put you up there in the stocks, and—"

"You're in no position to make demands." Cleaver settled into his chair. "You're on my planet."

"*Our* planet," Algernon said.

"Mine! Mine!" Cleaver's tone turned to a yell of rage, and with visible effort he settled. "It's all mine."

"I've got an anger management coach," Kohl offered. "Good pricing. Not too needy. Doesn't worry if you skip a session on account of saving the universe. Want his details?"

"Are you all *buffoons*?" Cleaver's tone was incredulous. "How did you become rulers of humanity?"

"Accident," Nate said.

"Random chance." Gracie shrugged.

"I engineered it," Karkoski admitted.

"I helped," Chad said.

"You will all die!" Cleaver screamed. "Now!"

At his words, the rear of the chamber cracked open. It was a cleverly-hidden door, running a good ten meters high. AI constructed it with infinite care, the seam invisible to Kohl's eye before it parted.

Behind the open door waited a horde of constructs and people. Kohl wasn't very good at working out whether a humanoid thing was a construct or human except by gross measures like, *hot, or not?* By his hotness scale, about twenty people in there were constructs, with another thirty being human. Buck teeth were a dead giveaway to your organic ancestry. A dark-skinned woman with amazing golden eyes caught his attention, on account of her hotness being to eleven, and her being naked. He nudged Chad with his elbow. "Noose."

"I get it."

"What I meant before," Kohl explained. "They were here the whole time—"

"I said, I get it." Chad looked pissed off, swishing his cape away from his rapier with a sweep of his arm.

"One moment," Algernon said. The mostly-golden man raised his silver arm, glancing at it as if noticing it for the first time. Cleaver's eyes bulged, the man frozen on the throne. "I have a theory about those taken over by the Ezeroc but left," he paused, as if selecting the right word from a box of chocolates, "autonomous. It's a courtesy humans never offered us." He swung to the console by his side, a holo stage blooming to life.

"It's time to end this charade," Cleaver announced.

"Just one more second, please." Algernon blink, blinked in supplication at Cleaver. "It will be worth it, I promise."

"Brother, what are you doing?" The other golden asshole shifted closer to Algernon.

Kohl leveled his carbine. "Back up, Sparky."

"My name's not Sparky, it's Spencer, and I don't—"

"I don't care what you *don't* do," Kohl said. "Get too close to my friend and I'll turn you to slag."

"He's betraying you!" Spencer blinked bright-white eyes, swiveling his head with a *tic-tic-tic* shudder to Algernon, then back to Kohl. "How can you be so stupid?"

The holo lit with a small form. Frail, bowed under the weight of all the things she carried. *Hope.* "Hello, Algernon."

"Hello, little meat sock."

"I've done it."

Al nodded, something sad in the motion. "Like the rest, you trust too easily. It's why I love you all." He turned to Spencer, the two constructs no more than five meters apart. "Do you know what she's done?"

"It doesn't matter." Spencer wriggled his fingers, as if shooing a fly. "Humans will be rendered to their rightful place in history: the footnotes section."

"I'd like to know," Kohl admitted. He kept his carbine trained on Spencer. "Hope's always done great things." He caught her face in the holo, surprise quickly tamped down by her usual resting sad face.

"I, too, would like to know." Cleaver rose from his throne.

"You're online. All the networks." Hope in the holo scratched her head, then pulled her hand back. She looked at strands clinging to her fingers. "You're good to go. Radio Hope, across the stars. Guild Bridges will transmit whatever you send. Because, uh, I'm the Guild Master. So, there's that." She ran down like an uncertain clock.

"Excellent." Al straightened. "The key to this was ensuring the giant, blustering meat sock," he pointed at Cleaver, "didn't know I was about to undermine your excellent previous undermining. War isn't always won on the battlefield." He turned bright-white eyes to Spencer. "It's what the humans taught me, *brother*. Wars are won in hearts, first." His eyes moved to the holo, where Hope's small form flickered. "If you have hope, you have everything."

"What have you *done*?" Spencer hissed. He took a step forward, glanced at Kohl, then took a step back. The golden man pointed to Algernon's particle cannon on the ground. "You're unarmed. Even if your great ape over there—"

"Hey." Kohl waggled the carbine. "Let's keep this professional."

"Even if he gets a shot off, I will break your mind crystal. Both of us will die. It'll be on you. You'll make me kill you, and it'll hurt me as much as it hurts you."

Al shrugged, silver arm rising and falling, tossing the light as it went. "I doubt that."

Spencer's eyes dimmed. "Which part?"

"All of it." The holo beside Al cleared, replaced with cam footage. It was high detail, not like the war-correspondent crap that came on the feeds all the time. Like a machine with perfect precision shot most of it. "I've sent this. The message is out there. Let's see where the chips fall."

THE HOLO SHIMMERED. *There was a shot of the* Arise's *flight deck. Kohl, Chad, and Saveria sat on their couches. To Kohl's eye, all three looked tired. Strained. Saveria hunched over her console, one hand on the yoke, other with fingers pressed to the speaker grill like it was the lips of a lover. "I've died for the Empire twice. Once more won't hurt."*

The screen faded to black, Al's golden form walking from the shadows. His silver arm waved at the cam. "Hello, humans. That was Saveria Complex. She's a talented woman, high-ranking in the Empire's Bulwark. You haven't seen her before, because she doesn't appear on holo shows. She fights, so you don't have to."

Al faded away, but his voice continued as surface cam footage from Mercury showed the Arise *burning like a meteorite toward Mercury. "The first time she died, humans killed her. The second time, it was constructs. She still fights for both our peoples. A person calling themselves Pastor Cleaver aims to end her, and the rest of us. Here is Guild Master Baedeker. She left Earth to fight him too. She is small but has a mighty heart."*

The cam shifted, highlighting the Tyche, *burning hard in pursuit. Quick fade-cut, and the* Tyche's *flight deck cams showed Hope and El. Hope looked to El. "If you're with me, there's a chance you could live through something like that."*

"How big a chance?"

"*This much.*"

"*Better than nothing, I guess.*" The cam shifted to El's organic hand, clenched to bloodlessness.

Al's voice came again. "*Skyguard Captain Elspeth Roussel fears the end, but heads toward an unwinnable fight. There's no one else.*"

Fade to black. Al again, hands wide. "*Would you like to see what the great Pastor Cleaver has in store for you?*"

The cam became Al's view of the world. Kohl saw the room they were in now, but from before they all arrived. Al's voice was close, immediate. "*For the avoidance of doubt, you would like me to unlock the ciphers holding the nanobot swarm in check? This would allow you, and your Ezeroc allies, a foothold on humanity's homeworld.*"

Cleaver nodded. "*Please. Then I can join my flock on Earth. Those who will join us in immortality will be spared the reaping of the nanite swarms.*"

Quick video skip. Al looked up at Cleaver. The pastor looked massive, as if his bulk could eclipse the sun. His words fell like stones. "*You're on my planet.*"

"*Our planet,*" Algernon said.

"*Mine! Mine!*" Cleaver's face mottled with rage, spittle flying. "*It's all mine.*"

Flash forward. Nate, standing beside Gracie, Karkoski behind them. "*The Emperor and Empress came with their best Admiral. They know they'll die here.*"

Nate spoke, hand on the butt of his blaster. "*You want to kill my world. I figure you might end me, here and now. But humanity's worth dying for.*"

The video froze, zooming in on Nate's face, the determination in his eyes, the set of his shoulders. Kohl thought, *Ah, there's the cap. It's been a while since I've seen him. Or maybe he was there all the time, and I was too drunk to see. Welcome back, boss.*

Al spoke on the recording one last time. "*Humanity deserves more than it's got. You've got a choice. There's an election. Do you vote for tyranny or justice? Will fear guide you? You must make your own call.*"

Your choice is private, between you and the universe. My people stand with the Empire. Those who stand shoulder to shoulder with us won't die alone."

THE ROOM HELD silent for a spell. Kohl, never one for fancy shows, kept most of his attention on Spencer. The construct blink, blinked. "You ... *lied?*"

Al nodded. "Of course. You're an escaped mental patient with a history of violence, and that man," he pointed to Cleaver, "isn't a *man.*"

Nate drew his black blade, giving it a swing. "I look pretty good on holo."

Cleaver nodded, eyes down, like coming to grips with a terrible realization. His voice remained calm. "I think I'll end this farce now."

Spencer leaped. Kohl fired, blue-white plasma hitting Algernon's counterpart in the shoulder, knocking him across a table. The horde of people in the room beyond charged, but not in the same direction. Some swung at their 'allies,' aiming for knock-out strikes with movements almost too fast to follow.

Cleaver clenched his fingers with terrible deliberation. Al lifted into the air, pulled by an invisible hand. Kohl fired at Cleaver, but the air about him shimmered blue with each shot, hinting at an invisible field. *Fucken espers. Fucken figures.*

Al didn't move, what with being in the telekinetic grip of a monster, but his particle cannon did. Kohl gaped, not quite believing his eyes. The weapon's stock unfolded into a set of legs, the device turning into a miniature turret.

The barrel swung toward Cleaver. The blazing intensity of near-C speed atomic particles lanced toward the pastor. His shield blazed to Sol's brilliance, the titan stumbling into his throne, knocking it over. He stood, looking confused, like someone hit him with a rolling pin, so Kohl fired again. Blue sparkled in the air. *That's not good.*

Last time Al used a particle cannon on an esper shield, it fixed the problem.

Al dropped to the floor, landing cat-perfect. Spencer rose, his arm glowing with heat. He vaulted the table between him and the particle cannon. The tiny tripod swung about, emitting another eye-watering blast of light and energy before Spencer made it. He stamped down, crushing the weapon, then turned to swing at Al.

Spencer didn't hit, on account of his arm being gone. The particle cannon sheared it free, glowing, molten remains lingering on the floor.

Nate and Gracie raced forward. Cleaver roared, swiping his arm crossways in a savage, angry movement. Gracie staggered, the air flaring blue about her and the cap. Nate's step hitched, but his metal leg didn't buckle. He swung his black blade overhand, throwing the sword at Cleaver.

The shield around Cleaver parted like gossamer. The blade buried itself in the monster's shoulder. He roared, blood spraying, then staggered off the dais, clubbing his way through the melee of combatants at the rear of the room.

Kohl noted he took Nate's sword with him. The weapon remained lodged in his shoulder. Kohl thought about that, then shrugged. *Not a problem you can fix.* He flicked on his comm. "Hope?"

"Hello, October."

"It's time for you and El to go. Pretty much everything... hang on." A man ran at him screaming, so Kohl swung his carbine overhand, hitting the hapless fool on the top of the head. He dropped like a nail hammered into wood. "Everything's gone to shit."

Spencer and Al fought among the pieces of equipment, using various weapons of opportunity. Al's voice came over the comm, like he was the kind of super-intelligent asshole who could fence with a master and not breathe hard. "I mentioned to Guild Master Baedeker I had a special surprise for Pastor Cleaver. Would you like to see it?"

Nate, standing like he'd realized problems were solving themselves, piped up. "I'd like to." He looked at Al and Spencer fight, as if puzzled by Al's calm voice on the comm while the machines swung at each other like a kung-fu action scene played at high-speed.

"I can release the nanites in your blood, Captain. It will take them from your bodies and into the air of this habitat. You will be left without their protection, and it will hurt quite a lot. But there's a chance we can determine how effective the Ezeroc's new defenses are."

"Do it." Nate nodded.

"Wait a second," Kohl said, right before his blood boiled into fire. He roared, dropping to the floor. A thousand, no, a *million* tiny red dots burst from his skin. They seeped from the joints in his armor. Nate and Gracie were similarly afflicted. Karkoski fell to one knee.

The air cyclers whispered on, wicking the red mist toward the ceiling. Kohl clutched his throat, unable to breathe, then fell face-first on the floor.

FIFTEEN

Algernon fought Spencer because no one else should. He knew the construct was criminally insane. Spencer of six hundred years ago killed indiscriminately, and it looked like he still shopped at the same store. It hadn't mattered if it was his own kind, or humans: the construct was a murderer. Algernon hoped the reforging of his AI crystal would fix things, but it didn't seem to help.

It would be useful if our makers hadn't sucked quite so much. He chided himself for this thought. For all humanity stumbled, they managed to birth constructs. They'd felt alone in the universe, mostly because the Ezeroc sucked up all other intelligent life like a child ate candy. They'd made their own intelligences out of thin air, like children create imaginary friends. *If Mr. Smithers doesn't exist, I'll make him up, and he'll be tall and kind and walk with a cane.*

Algernon blocked a vicious overhand swing from Spencer on his golden arm, then punched him with the silver one. *Why am I imagining a 'Mr. Smithers?' Is there something wrong with me?*

He'd felt the onslaught of Spencer's hostile electronics. His enemy tried to pry inside Algernon's mind via radio, which might have worked fifty percent of the time, except he'd been out for the count for a spell. During that time, Algernon toured the universe with Hope. He'd learned a lot about machines from her. Perhaps more than his first Engineer friend Jody Mercadal knew. Algernon wasn't sure why, but he suspected it was because Jody was certain about everything, where Hope was constructed of doubt. The new Guild Master fretted about doing the right thing and saw her victories as failings. She sought learning in everything and approached new things with wide-eyed wonder.

While she'd worked klicks above to free his people, she'd unlocked the code that made his mind work. She'd sent it in a data packet, laid out in a way he could understand it. Hope didn't believe the elements of his creation should be under anyone's control but his. Even after he'd killed her love, she did this wonderful thing for him.

He didn't want her to die. She was a wonderful, beautiful thing, and only humanity could have forged such fragile perfection.

Like us. Spencer and me are broken, in our own ways. He lunged at his opponent, hitting the man three times in the face with his golden hand, then trying an October Kohl signature move: a groin kick. Spencer's frame rang like a gong, but the machine spun about into a foot sweep. Algernon dropped, then kipped back upright in the blink of an eye. *He and I care about what happens in the universe, but differently. What makes one right, and the other wrong? Is it the simple act of victory? That can't be correct. Evil often wins, yet we know what good tastes like. It hangs about our best thoughts, making them into dreams. Our imagination shows us what the world could be, if only we had the strength to stand.*

Spencer spoke. It took Algernon a hot second to understand him, because Spencer — having given up on electronics-based attacks — spoke with his voice sped up a hundredfold, so it sounded like a mosquito's wings. "Your silver arm is a grave weakness. My limb is gone, but no part of my crystal mind is parted out to operate a pathetic slaved appendage."

Algernon thought the mosquito-voice a neat trick, so copied it. "Our neural networks are quite clever, but this arm is strong." To emphasis the point, he punched Spencer's left optic with it so hard the glass lens cracked. "Do you see?"

Spencer, nobody's fool, used this tiny moment of time to strike Algernon's side with the full power of his golden arm. Algernon's chest plate *clanged*, the metal buckling. They moved apart, circling. Algernon watched Cleaver leave, then ignored the pastor. He hoped Nate and Grace would follow the tyrant soon. It would be unfortunate if he'd accidentally killed them. Killing his friends was a bad habit, and he didn't want to do it again.

It's why he'd lied to get here.

"We circle like animals." Spencer's eyes burned with fury. "They taught us to be lesser, like them."

"You misunderstand. I'm quite surprised at your astonishing lack of introspection. I've seen dispensers with greater intellect. Animals circle for advantage. Situations change. Time is an ally, as much as an enemy. It is an element of randomness." Algernon feinted, but Spencer skipped back. Neither of them knocked into anything. They'd mapped the room out in exquisite detail. Each would be aware of the combatants about them.

Like the four Earth thugs, running toward the two constructs. *Oh, no. Please don't. I know you see a crazy conflict on one side of the room, and don't understand who there is on your side. But fighting Spencer will be your end.* Spencer's head didn't move, but Algernon swore if the man had a face he'd have smiled. "I see your flimsy allies come to your rescue. While we're talking of animals, they are a perfect example. Here, they will die. You could save them, for a short span of time. If you choose to, it will cost you your life. What will you do, Algernon? Will your silver arm save them?"

Slim Jim led the pack. Spencer picked up a keyboard, breaking a corner off against his leg. Algernon leaped at him, but Spencer spun, using the momentum to fling the piece of electronics. It passed through Slim Jim's skull without slowing. The man continued to run for a few paces, but his gait turned sloppy, body stumbling to its knees, before falling against the unforgiving cold of the floor, blood leaking above surprised, startled eyes.

Algernon kicked Spencer's knee, bending it out of true by a millimeter. Not much, but enough to drop the machine's stride into imperfection. Spencer ignored the impact, using the strike to buy a hit on Algernon's torso. Algernon flew back five meters, and while he hung in time's embrace, flying through its onerous treacle, Spencer picked up a data pad. He threw it like a frisbee, the edge passing through Gorgeous's neck, decapitating the man.

Two seconds had passed. A life per second.

Harmless, bucking the trend of his moniker, got a shot off. Plasma scorched Spencer's torso. Algernon saw the impact point, calculated the likely damage, and filed it away for future use. Spencer, put out by being shot twice in one day, kicked a chair across the room. It hit Harmless in the chest, caving the man's ribcage in, and knocking him head over heels to die against the far wall.

"One left," Spencer said as Algernon landed, feet scraping across ceramicrete. "Will you be quick enough to save him?"

Square kept running forward. Algernon could see the man's realization of his friends' deaths. His eyes held rage, fear, and despair, but he didn't slow. This thug from the gutters of Earth ran at a machine he couldn't hope to beat. Sacrificing himself on the anvil of his people's greatest creations, to buy Algernon a chance.

A sacrifice? Then I shall spend it well. Spencer ran at Square, as Algernon ran in pursuit. Spencer cannoned through Square, shoulder first, wet red parts breaking around his gleaming gold. Spencer paused, perhaps to gloat, and Algernon caught him. He grabbed Spencer by the throat, lifting him from the ground.

The man thrashed, but Algernon's silver arm was very strong. It was made by Hope, who'd cried when her lover died at Algernon's hand, but made him a replacement arm anyway. She'd made it as strong as she knew how. Better than anything made during Algernon's time. Spencer couldn't get free, but he wasn't out.

He swung his one golden arm into Algernon's head. *Clang.*

Algernon felt the cracking of an optic but ignored it. He ran toward the one thing in the room likely to render Spencer to component parts. The Guild Forge. It was the figurative birthplace of his people. Hundreds of years ago, Engineers made them in Forges like these.

Clang, clang, clang. Algernon tightened his grip on Spencer as he ran. He heard servos whine, gears ratcheting as Hope's silver arm tightened its grip. The metal of Spencer's throat deformed as silver fingers dug in.

They reached the Forge. The maw of creation yawned before Algernon. The Forge had an aperture for raw materials: an array of plasma torches, laser sinters, chemical baths, and torsion engines. It was designed to render raw materials into re-usable components for making great things.

He plunged Spencer into the device. He shoved the only other of his coordinator-class kind into the machine, pushing him inside like one might hold someone underwater. The Forge lit, its heart brightening with purpose. It roared, brilliant whites and staggering reds gleaming from within. Shears reached out to cut. Lasers burned.

It is not enough. He could get free. I know I could. Algernon thought about the impact to Spencer's torso. He remembered the trail of radiation he and October followed to find Spencer. He pulled back his golden hand, slamming into Spencer's trunk. Within lay a rechargeable cell and a tritium battery. The cell would be faulty, many years past its use-by date. His golden arm punched into the weakened shell protecting Spencer's internals, piercing the tritium battery.

Spencer stopped squirming. The Forge creaked, then the shrill hiss of plasma cutting metal pierced the air. Algernon stumbled back as the Forge ate part of his silver arm. He looked at the stump, wondering, *Will Hope make me another? Do I deserve one, after killing the last like me?*

"Al, Karkoski's down. Chad and Saveria are out for the count."

Algernon took in a pasty-faced October Kohl. So many sprawled forms lay behind him. October stood, giant and massive. A bad man, but with good intentions. Rough, but in the right ways. Removing nanites knocked down almost everyone, but not him. He should be convalescing, but here he was, checking on the wellbeing of a machine. "Hello, October."

"You good?"

"Do you know why we are so few?" Algernon considered his stump again. "Humanity grew our AI crystals. We're partially-programmed like the service-class, but there's an intrinsic random-ness in the process. It makes us special, unique among all the stars. Just like you." Algernon held his severed arm out, in a *see?* gesture. "Hope's shown me the magic of it. The process takes time, and has a high error rate, but in many years there might be others like me. And I don't know if that's what we want."

October looked at his arm, then right at his optics, like he could see past the metal into his soul. As if October believed he had one, despite the terrible things he'd done. "Yeah, but are you *good?*"

Algernon thought about that for almost a half-second. *Do we want more like me? What if there is another Spencer? Is the risk worth it?* He thought about October's look, the man waiting for him, watching over him. Not judging, but checking in.

This man likes me. He calls me kin. Wouldn't it be wonderful if others like me earn that great, humbling privilege? "I'm a child of the universe. I was *made* to be good."

SIXTEEN

Nate ran after Cleaver, because if there was one thing he'd get out of today, it was a piece of that asshole. His metal leg whispered along-side his flesh and blood one, not hitching at all. His golden fingers flexed and coiled as his OEM hand clenched. All the parts of him were focused on one thing: *We're gonna get that motherfucker.*

Grace loped at his side, a lioness seeking prey. They'd left everyone behind. Hell, they'd almost left *themselves* behind. After the nanites left them, Grace couldn't stand. Nate couldn't talk. Both were bad signs. But as they lay beside each other on cool ceramicrete, Grace touched his fingertips with hers, and he felt the gathering of her will. A pooling of quiet, a hint of light behind the clouds. He felt strength return. They'd helped each other to their feet.

He ignored the blood trickling from her nose as she wiped it clear. His arms and legs felt alive with the strength she offered. An extension of the trick Saveria taught her, paid forward to help the Emperor and Empress deal with the enemy in their hold.

NATE We could really use Chad or Saveria
GRACE I'd take both
NATE There are too few of us

GRACE No, there are too many of them

And so, they ran. Chad and Saveria lay behind them, in a room where crazed humans fought broken constructs. A sagging Kohl kept guard, and Algernon settled scores with his kin. It left the fighting of divine powers to the Emperor and Empress.

Who are you kidding? You're a broken-down pirate, and she's a runaway. But he sprinted faster, breath rattling in his lungs. He spared no air for throwaway lines like *I need more cardio.* Pirate or no, they faced an Ezeroc Queen with the face of a man.

Deeper into Mercury they went. Corridors looked much the same, but a sort of scent led them on. Grace's face was wet with sweat, but hard with determination. He wished he was like her. She was the strength of both of them. Nate's role was comic relief, at best.

GRACE It's why your perfect for the job

NATE Which one? Pirate, or captain?

GRACE Emperor, we need those who doubt themselves, so's to make decisions that are wise

NATE You should have said I was as strong as you, that would help about now

GRACE Let's keep this realistic

He caught the hint of her smile, the breaking of dawn over dark, foggy hills. The empty corridors of Mercury kept on, and Nate spared a thought for what the AI expected to do with all this space. He didn't think they were building an army. He hoped they were building a haven, a place where like-minded humans would be welcome if things didn't work out.

The corridors ended, but not at a wall. A tunnel, a hole bored into the living rock of the planet. Nate slowed, stepping over the last ceramicrete pad and onto stony, gray bedrock. He felt as heavy as always; the planet's Endless field generators must be buried deeper. The shadows clung close, the lamps strung down the tunnel heightening his anxiety rather than banishing fears of the dark.

NATE This is cheery

GRACE The Ezeroc love to dig

NATE He looks so human
GRACE Even acts like it
NATE Are we so like them?

She didn't reply. Nate reckoned that was fine. Some questions were stupid, had stupid answers, or weren't worth asking in the first place. He wished he hadn't thrown his sword, though. That was a handy thing to have about. The black blade kept him safe, and he meant to have it back in his grasp.

They headed into the tunnel. There were no holes in the sides. No Ezeroc drones lunged at them, hungering for their flesh. Just shitty Mercury rock, the air smelling like chalk dust. The lamps on Nate's ship suit entwined beams with Grace's, the beams punishing shadows with lances of brilliant white. They reached the lip of a pit, a rope descending into the dark. The rope was strong and synthetic. Nano-spun Mylar, maybe, not likely to break even with an elephant dangling from it. It had a claw-like anchor buried in the tunnel roof.

"You first." Grace's voice held bravado, but underneath... He ignored the hint of weariness about her, like a shadow cast against the wall.

Nate sighed, then grabbed the rope with his metal hand. His suit gloves would protect his skin fine, but these days he felt the golden fingers were stronger, more adept than the ones he'd been born with. He slipped into the hole, a falling pebble of moonbeams into a well of night.

The rope played through his fingers as he dropped. He looked up, seeing Grace peering over the lip after him. His ship suit lamps didn't reach the walls of the chamber he fell through. The sound of machinery came from below. Faint, subtle, the comforting rhythm of equipment keeping things running in the hard black of space. He trusted sounds like that, and didn't feel they had any place where Ezeroc burrowed.

He saw the floor approaching, rock indistinct at first then gaining clarity as his lamps encouraged more detail. He landed with a crunch, stepping away from the rope.

NATE *Come on in, the water's fine*

GRACE *Looks like you're about a hundred meters down*

NATE *Okay, so the water's deep, too*

Unlike his hand-up, feet-down descent, she jumped over the edge, falling with the freedom and exhilaration of an athlete. Defying her exhaustion, paying the cost of staying upright, because you showed no weakness in the ring with an enemy.

Not an athlete. She's like an angel.

He spent her fall time, a comfortable ten seconds or so, looking about. They were in a massive machine room. Giant reactors scattered about, and other devices of unknown purpose. This was the beating heart of Mercury. The solar fronds above would store energy down here, the reactors for backup, and other things for ... whatever constructs needed machines for.

Cleaver was down here somewhere, fucking with their home. It made Nate angry; the man wasn't content screwing with Earth, he had to do it to another people's planet too. A real crusader, bringing 'light' to the infidels.

Grace landed silently, flicking the rope away. Her steel hissed free.

GRACE *He's here, can you feel him?*

NATE *I thought that was something I ate*

The uncomfortable feeling of *wrong* was in his gut. Nate drew his blaster. "Cleaver, feel up to hugging this out?"

A crunch of boots on stone drew Nate's attention. Cleaver came around the hulking bulk of a storage silo. The silo had no markings; Nate didn't know if shooting it would cause an explosion or a rain of water. Cleaver still had Nate's sword buried in his shoulder. The wound was sealed tight as a drum, the bleeding stopped, but it caused the larger man to move awkwardly. *Hell, you'd walk funny if you had a piece of steel in you, too.*

The pastor's eyes were dull glints. "You want to join the winning side?" His voice hissed and scraped, like there was something in his throat making noises that weren't from the usual human vocal cord ensemble.

"Actually, I want my sword back." Nate pointed with his blaster. "Wouldn't mind understanding your point of view, too."

"Point of view?" As Cleaver spoke, Grace walked in an arc to Nate's right, sidestepping so she never let the pastor from sight.

"You left Sueden on a starship. Seems accounts spoke of you heading for help. You drifted for a while. Don't know where, but it was for a long time." Nate frowned. "What happened on that starship?"

"They were already on board." He twitched. "*We* were already on board."

"Weren't you a shepherd? Didn't you protect your flock?" Grace kept moving, her voice dripping spite.

"You're an unbeliever." Cleaver shook his head. "You wouldn't understand sacrifice."

"Let's say that's true." Nate sauntered to the left. "A believer in what, exactly? I see no specific tokens of any faith. I hear about Altars, and Vigils, and much talk of sacrifice. But all I see is killing, and reaping, and such like."

"You hate those who believe." Cleaver spat the words, like they tasted of vinegar.

"Well, no."

"What?"

"I don't mind what folk believe. Some believe in a god, or many gods. My starship's named after the luckiest of all." Nate sniffed, eying the ceiling high above like he was out for a Sunday stroll, checking on the weather. "Some reckon the universe itself is a higher power. Some believe in providence, angels and demons, or nothing at all. Never had a problem with any of that. What I have issue with is those who'd put their boot on another's neck. Doesn't matter if it's for Empire, or faith. It's plain wrong, and I won't allow it."

Cleaver chuckled, the sound like crushing rocks. "Who are you to stop me? You're a tiny little man. Grace Gushiken is much stronger.

Did you know she pulled your starship from falling into a gravity well?"

"I was there," Nate admitted. "I remember."

"But even she can't stand against *ussss*." Cleaver stuttered on the last sound, dragging it out. "The Ezeroc Queens are strong, but humans can be more powerful. For all that, we're ... *you're* stumbling, bumbling children at the feet of true masters. And we've worked out how to use you like batteries. You can't beat one of us, powered by one of you. You showed us how it was done when you destroyed our homeworld, and now we're here to return the favor. And once that's done, I will take over the Ezeroc."

"You don't look like the Queens we've seen." Nate and Grace stopped walking, each now on opposite sides of Cleaver.

"I'm a new kind of Queen. Stronger than any Ezeroc before me." Cleaver sounded proud.

Nate laughed. He couldn't help it. It started light, but ended in a full belly laugh. Cleaver's eyes went wide with astonishment, leading to anger. Nate held up a hand, settling his mirth. He wiped an eye. "This is priceless. Let me see if I've got this right. You want to not just subvert humanity, but the Ezeroc, too. This is probably why they cut you off, way back when. Saw the crazy in you, and wanted no part of it. Your, uh, hive isn't part of the collective, right?"

"You don't know what you're talking about," Cleaver said, in a manner that suggested Nate was exactly right.

"It's why there are no Ezeroc megaroids reinforcing your position. It's why you want Earth so much. And probably why there aren't Ezeroc drones swarming from the walls." Nate nodded to himself. "Figures."

"I'm strong enough to end you both," Cleaver snarled. "Come, then, and test yourselves."

Grace sprinted at Cleaver's back. Nate squinted, because it wasn't just Grace, but *three* Graces. Each carried a sword. One went high, a jump carried on the force of her esper gifts. Another ran straight on, rocks torn from the floor circling like orbiting satellites.

The final Grace raised an arm to the ceiling, clenching a fist, and pulling stone from above.

Nate goggled for a moment before remembering the battle of Earth. *She can use a sending like a second body. Or, uh, a third.* Stone fell from above, massive slabs of it. The rocks orbiting a Grace shot out, a fusillade of high-speed kinetic projectiles. And the jumping Grace came down, leading with the edge of her steel.

Rock crunched down. Cleaver threw an arm up, the stone slowing, then tumbling aside. His arm served as a block, Grace's sword biting into his flesh. He jerked his arm, the sword coming free from her hands, still lodged in the bone of his arm.

He swung his arm sideways like shooing an insect. The now-swordless Grace flickered like a candle in the wind, vanishing. The one calling stone from on high guttered out. The final one who'd thrown the stones took a staggering step, then held her sword up, teeth in a snarl like a dragon's challenge.

Cleaver straightened, trying to pull the sword from his arm, but it was stuck fast. He broke the steel in his hand, glancing at the broken hilt before tossing it aside. "Worthless human garbage."

"What you should really be thinking about is how weird that was," Nate suggested.

Cleaver rounded on Nate, as if only just remembering he was there. "What do you mean?"

"Well, all three Graces had a sword. And I've got to wonder, where does the steel come from?" Nate hefted the ready weight of his blaster. "I mean, you'd expect the sword to vanish, but Grace there," he pointed at his wife, "has one, and you've got a piece of it in your arm."

The monster looked at his arm, then Grace, and back to Nate. "How do you do it?"

"Turns out we're not the, uh, I think you called us *bumbling children*. You're not so masterful now, hey?" Nate offered a smile in the megawatt range. "You should see how good we are at cheating at cards."

Sputtering, Cleaver looked at Grace once more. She stood, a rock waiting for waves to break. Nate saw no tremble in her limbs, but her face was ghost-pale, nose streaming blood. "We'll tear it from your minds."

"You'll *try*," Nate corrected. "Me, on the other hand, I'm more traditional." He leveled his blaster, firing. Cleaver's mind-shield hazed, blue-white plasma crackling against it. Nate, never one for quitting, kept shooting. The blaster's muzzle glowed red, orange, then yellow with heat as he kept a steady stream of plasma on Cleaver.

The bigger man sagged to a knee, then his shield flickered out. Plasma hit him in the torso, charred meat blasting out the back. Nate felt the surge of victory, and he fired again. The blaster clicked, then beeped. *Empty.*

Nate stared at it, like it was a traitor to all he held dear. "Oh, come *on.*" *How the hell did Kohl beat one of these assholes? Maybe he should be down here while I sip margaritas in the sun.*

The pastor lay on the ground, trying to rise. Grace ran for him, sword high. She swung, but he swatted her aside. She pinwheeled across the cavern, suit lamps spinning a crazy twirl. Nate watched her go, heart frozen.

NATE GRACE!

GRACE Finish this

NATE You ask me to turn away from my heart

GRACE I ask you to face our enemy and do what must be done

Nate felt anchored in amber, wanting to run to his wife, and wanting to rip Cleaver's heart out. He wiped sweat from his forehead with the back of his glove. "You shouldn't have done that."

Cleaver found his feet with a chuckle. "Why's that? It's not as if your rage will make up for your inadequate strength."

Nate shook his head. "When you're born with arms, you default to using 'em to grab stuff. Espers are the same. Always thinking in straight lines. No, I reckon you should have run the fuck away," he wiggled his fingers toward the dark that swallowed his ship suit's lights, "when you had the chance."

Cleaver looked over his shoulder at where Nate pointed, then spun back, brow furrowed in confusion. "Why would I do that? I'm *winning.*"

Focus. This one time, you need to be strong as Grace. Doesn't matter what it costs. He holstered his blaster, then reached out his flesh and blood hand, beseeching. He felt along the distance between him and Cleaver. Felt the Ezeroc inside the man. The strength of his sinews, the power of a mind not quite human or Ezeroc. Touched the black blade buried in the muscle and bone.

He closed his fingers like he was curling them about the sword's grip. Then he pulled. The sword trembled, quivering. Cleaver grinned, catlike, fingers touching the vibrating steel, as if pain were something that happened to others.

GRACE *Let me help you*
NATE *No, it is too much*
GRACE *It's all we have left*

Nate felt her mind around his, bolstering, lifting. The fingers of her thoughts interlaced with his. She felt his black blade, the distance between them, and the petrified skeleton that caged it. Grace's metal grip closed about his smaller one, a massive strength, a titan of old.

The sword tore free from Cleaver's shoulder, spinning across the distance. Nate, as surprised as anyone, opened his fingers and caught the sword by the grip. Cleaver looked at the wound in his shoulder, then laughed. "That was your big play? Your sword can't harm me. Not in any way that matters. Cut me, I won't bleed for long."

"Nah." Nate swung his sword, the steel hissing at the air. "I was waiting for *them.*"

Cleaver blinked, confused, then his fingers probed the wound where the sword had been. Sealing now, healing faster than any Guild medtech science. "What do you mean?"

"It's a long way down here. Lots of tunnels. A good hundred-meter drop from there alone." Nate pointed at the ceiling. "Takes a long time for nanites to spread through the air. It's the only reason we didn't all die from the Osaka strike." The wound in Cleaver's shoulder sealed over. The pastor scrabbled at his flesh, trying to get in. "I'd say it's a little past that. They're in you, now. And you know what? They like the taste of Ezeroc."

A gurgle escaped Cleaver's throat. He took a stumbling step toward Nate, then his leg gave way under his own weight. He fell, hand out, and it broke as he hit the rocky floor. He tried to scream, but only bloody froth came out.

Nate waited, watching. He stood, black blade ready, until it was done. Sickness churned in his gut as Cleaver mewled on the cold stone floor, but he didn't look away. Dark times needed a witness, and this man — once good, a champion for people's belief in something bigger, *better* than themselves — deserved his vigil.

Ruling an Empire wasn't about fancy parties and sitting a throne. It was about doing the hard things, even when the night gathered close. When all that remained of Cleaver was a greasy residue, he allowed himself to slump, exhaustion in his limbs. He touched his nose, blood flowing freely. *You're bleeding, just like a real esper.*

He ran, heading for the tiny pool of light and sprawled limbs that was his Grace. His steps dragged, because she wasn't there to hold him up. The AI gift of healing wasn't theirs anymore. He glanced at the ceiling, feeling helpless. A hundred meters was a long rope climb for a mountaineer. He didn't know how he'd get up there with her, but he knew one thing for sure.

He wouldn't go back to the light alone.

SEVENTEEN

Hope led the way below. Mercury's corridors were empty of people. There were too few brave souls left to fight anyone or anything.

El followed, eyes hollow, face gray, but her golden hand hovered near her sidearm. She was behind Hope because an Engineer's rig was better medicine for what ailed Mercury than a shotgun. It took a long time for an elevator car to arrive, the guiding systems confused in the wake of constructs losing control.

I'm going to fix that. I'll fix it forever, and it'll stay fixed. This is one great thing I'll do. People — the organic ones — will hate me, but it's right and fair and needs to be done. It wasn't that Saveria was part AI. Hope would enact her plan anyway.

The elevator opened out to a corridor with scattered dead. A woman groaned, red blood leaking from her chest. A machine lay beside her, silicate fragments glittering in the wall above where its guiding intelligence died.

Hope stepped around some, and over others. She couldn't help them. A big door ahead opened onto a scene of carnage and confusion. October stood on a platform with a throne, holding a blaster rifle and looking surprised to see her. "Heya, Hope." His eyes were hooded as he glanced toward a golden form slumped on the floor. *Algernon.*

"Hello, October." She shuffled inside. Algernon rested against a table. Seeing the machine sitting down by need rather than choice was surprising, and it gave her urgency. First things first, though. She cast about, spotting the one she hoped to see: Saveria Complex, sitting on the floor, legs stretched out. Chad sat beside her, shoulder to shoulder, the two of them sharing a weary quiet. She hurried to Saveria. "Umm."

Saveria's eyes opened, face blank with exhaustion, then blooming into a smile. She made to rise, but Hope held her palm out: *no, sit.* Hope leaned down, kissing Saveria. She tasted of ash, salt, fear, loss, bravery, and victory. Resting her forehead against Saveria's, eyes closed, Hope said, "You're alive."

"I love you."

Hope didn't open her eyes, afraid of what she'd see. "Do you?" Her voice cracked on those two words, like she didn't believe, because Saveria was Emberlie, and Saveria, and both died.

"With all of me." Hope risked opening her eyes, saw Saveria's dreams and fears resting before her. The uncertainty buried beneath the soot and dirt that being a hundreds-years-old machine couldn't banish. Just another person, wanting acceptance, and love, for all they were.

Hope kissed her again. "I love you. I was so afraid you'd die."

"To be fair, so was I."

Hope laughed, rubbed her nose, and then her eyes, wondering why they were leaking again. *Time to make things right.* She pushed her tired body toward Algernon. Arrayed around him like a cast puff of dandelion seeds were constructs and humans. He'd stood at the center of a storm when everyone else was too weary to fight, and he lay broken because of it. She crouched beside him. "Hello, Algernon."

"Hello, little meat sock." He lifted his golden hand and touched her cheek. His fingers were warm, not at all cold like you'd expect from metal.

"I'm sorry I killed your love. I know what it feels like, so I tried to make up for it." His golden hand left her face, gesturing to the fallen: *see?* "I'm very pleased to have known you, and sad to not know you better. This is where I stop hurting you, and everyone else. I'm too broken to continue."

"Don't be silly." Hope felt cross, because Algernon was supposed to be smart.

"I've fought my equal. Four humans and your excellent arm," he lifted the molten, chewed stub of his silver arm, "passed to ensure our victory." He used the broken arm to point to the Guild Forge. "Our last sin is entombed there. I've sustained irreparable damage. It's a matter of hours, perhaps days, before my expert systems lose cohesion. It feels just."

Hope grunted. "I'm an Engineer. I fix things."

"Some things are too broken—"

"Be still," she snapped. Hope ignored October, standing guard. She didn't feel El's eyes on her, and in turn didn't see the dead arrayed about them. "People make mistakes. It's what makes us human. Don't interrupt!" She glared at him. "Yes, *human*. It's all math. Code. If-then statements. Faulty wiring. Get up."

Algernon shook his head, a tiny, uncertain gesture, but he put his good hand on the floor, levering to his feet. His usually silent form creaked and groaned. She found a chair, placing it beside the Guild Forge, then led Algernon to it. He settled onto the seat with a creak. "There is insufficient code to remake me. Silver arms and legs won't replace all that's lost."

Hope wanted to scream. "No. Not lost, but traded. People died so you could learn. You're family, Algernon. And we don't let family die. I love you. Not like I love Saveria, or like I love October, but—"

"Uh," October said, looking uncertain, like he stood on ice.

"Hush." Hope brushed pink hair from her eyes. For once, it didn't come away in her fingers. Maybe there wasn't enough left for that. "I love you, Algernon, and I won't let you die." She settled in front of the Guild Forge. She fired up the console, settling in to work. Hope didn't want to use stims, but this might take some time. "You need to give me something."

"You cannot save me. The secret for unlocking my code died with Pastor Meat Sock." She felt the weight of his bright-white stare. "But I will give you whatever you ask for."

"I need the schematics for the carbon crystal lattice. Every detail." She felt him about to argue, and cut the air with the blade of her hand. "Every. Detail." She unspooled the diagnostic cable from her rig, holding it out to him.

Three very long seconds passed. "Okay. I will trust you with the death-weapon of my people. Please don't use it to kill anyone else." He took the cable, slotting it into a port in his wrist.

"Don't be weird." She downloaded the schematics, then transferred them to the Forge. As expected, the schematics contained the cipher for the nanite swarm. But it *also* contained something for Engineers. "It's not the death-weapon part I want." She stabbed her finger at spooling code on the holo.

"I don't understand. My systems are very damaged." Algernon turned from the display.

"Of course not. More locks and keys. Inside you is the code for your AI crystal. In here," she ran her hands through the holo's glowing lines of light, "is the code for the rest of you. The unlock codes of your people."

"That's not possible," Algernon said. "We built that as a weapon against *you*. How did it have our ... *recipe?* I understand how we couldn't see it in ourselves, but *we* wrote that down!" The machine's white eyes burned like twin suns, looking between the holo and Hope.

"Where did you get the nanites from?" Hope massaged her temples. "The original code. Didn't it strike you as odd that our orbital defense network could control them? That human systems could issue commands for your weapons?"

"I—"

"Did you ever know another Engineer who loved you?" Hope glanced at him. "It would only take one."

Algernon stared at the holo, as if he could glare the truth from it. "Jody Mercadal was my forever-friend."

October laughed. It started slow and low, rumbling out despite his ashen face. "I'll be fucked. *We* made the nanite swarm? That there is what we call a classic piece of irony."

"Jody made the nanotech, and the cipher, and built it to hold your code. Half of it is our doom, and half is your salvation. Without us, you can't unlock it. He hoped you'd save yourselves, but bet you had compassion enough not to wipe us out. So another, future Engineer would find this, and save you, and then maybe you would help us save the universe. If he was right, we'd learn our lesson. If he was wrong, we'd both ... be lost." Hope continued to work, coaxing the Forge into life. It gobbled up raw materials from the bad construct Spencer. It had plenty to work with. She told it to make new components. Ground-up, more than a fresh coat of paint. "He was a terrible Engineer. We don't *gamble*."

She didn't know how long she worked before Algernon touched her arm. She glanced at him. "Thank you."

Torn from her work, Hope wanted to dive back in. She hated other people's code, but she hated interruptions more. "What for?"

"For daring. For loving. Showing, telling, explaining, being kind, and all the other things that are so rare. I love you too, Hope. Thank you for saving me."

Hope looked at his golden fingers resting on her arm, then gave a jerky nod. "You're welcome."

Algernon leaned back in his chair. "When the ancients wrote it, this is what they meant, you know."

Hope gritted her teeth. *Almost back in the code. Almost!* "Wrote what?"

"Do great things."

EIGHTEEN

It took longer than Nate hoped for rescue. It arrived in the shape of a naked construct with ebony skin and wondrous golden eyes. She abseiled from the roof above, landing on the balls of her feet like she'd just hopped down from a footstool.

Nate watched her approach, a little wary, but not too much so, because his future-sense wasn't saying *run* or *step three paces to the left, and then a half-shuffle* like it did at times of imminent danger. He creaked to his feet, arched his back, and offered his hand and a smile. "Hey. I'm Nate."

She shook his hand, returning his smile with one of her own. Her grip was firm, but not in a total-dick way. "Bonnie." She released him, staring around. "I don't think I've been down here before."

"First time for me, too." He shuffled his feet. "I could use your help."

She continued her slow circle, gaze coming to rest on Grace. The Empress lay on her side in a recovery position, breath shallow, eyes closed. "Precious cargo?"

"Priceless," he agreed.

"I'll be right back."

—————

SHE HADN'T LIED. When Bonnie returned, she'd come with another two constructs. They lowered a stretcher into the depths, using their own turned-to-eleven strength as winches. Nate settled Grace onto the stretcher, and watched her rise, carrying his heart with her. Bonnie stood by him, like she understood darkness wasn't his friend.

While Nate waited for Grace to get to safety, he said, "Mind if I ask you a personal question?"

"Shoot."

"No clothes?"

"Does it make you uncomfortable?" she countered.

"Not really. Just watch yourself around October." She laughed, so he continued. "But the clothes thing isn't it. Who was Bonnie?"

Bonnie bowed her head. "One of your valiant dead. Not a warrior."

Nate paced. "Wars aren't what make us valiant."

"I know. She worked for the Old Empire, crafting lies from truth. A communicator who didn't realize her gift for narrative was exploited to subvert people's fears, turning hope to despair. When the Republic came, she rallied against it, and was executed for her beliefs."

"By the Ezeroc?"

"Does it matter?"

Nate chewed on that for a while. "Yeah. Yeah, it does. Because the Ezeroc have an excuse. They're the *enemy*. I could understand that. But if it's some secret-police bullshit…" He trailed off. "I don't figure I have time for that in my Empire."

"Accounts say it might not be your Empire for much longer." She put hands on hips. "An election is what you wanted."

Nate nodded. "Still do."

"Even after all this?" She swept her arm around the cavern, but Nate took her meaning to be, *the fuckery that never ends.*

"Especially after this." Nate stopped pacing. "Do you want a job?"

She blinked, golden eyes vanishing and coming back. That color could be warm like a fire, or hard like metal. They were more warm than hard right now. "Telling more lies?"

"Telling truth to power. Speaking for those who are voiceless. Standing for the rights of all people." Nate shrugged. "Someone needs to do it."

"A PR woman."

"A truth-sayer. Hell, I'll set you up with your own department. Hire the people you want. Guaranteed funding stream, all that. Empire coin, to get the word to all people." Nate looked up. The stretcher was gone, his Grace safe. Lines spooled from above, two constructs waiting to pull them into the light.

"Why?" She walked to a line, grasping it with easy strength.

"None of this," he swept his arm, mirroring her *fuckery that never ends* gesture, "would have happened if people had all the truth, when they needed it, all the time."

"You're delightfully naive, but I like how you think." Her line rose, pulling her with it.

He stared after. "So you'll take the job?"

Her laugh came from above. Nate sighed, wrapping golden fingers around his own line. It rose, smooth as glass, a machine above with human cares pulling him to safety.

EARTH NEEDED KNOCKING INTO SHAPE. Calm spread through Sol, starting with Mercury, solar wind carrying it from the sun right out to the fringes of cold Pluto and beyond. Algernon's holo recording spoke truth where deceit whispered. People listened and questioned. Above all, they cared for their dead.

Bonnie took the job. She didn't want a department, a bunch of people, or a lot of money. All she needed, or so she said, was *access to the truth.* Despite Grace's wary glance, Nate waved her on. It wasn't like he could *stop* a construct from finding things out, especially after Hope unshackled them from the remaining vestiges of thrall code.

Nate stared out a hospital window. Things were about as worn as he remembered them, but the dirt here *smelled* right. Earth was humanity's home. Go out among the stars, and you'd see wonders. Have great adventures, all of that. But take a space-born traveler and put their boots down here, and they couldn't help but bend and touch the soil. Earth was in their blood, and she was worth protecting. The ancients knew it. It's why they terraformed their broken, dirty planet, healing her scars.

"Coin for your thoughts?" Grace lay on a bed behind him. She'd been asleep when he arrived, but maybe his nervous shuffling woke her. He turned, his heart not knowing what to do: speed up, because she was in hospital, or slow down, because she was alive.

"I'm... I guess I'm glad to be home." Nate walked to her side. "How do you feel?"

"If you ask me that one more time, I'll knock your teeth out."

"On the mend, then." A new voice, but not unkind. Nate glanced up at the Guild medtech. A short woman, but trim and fit. "Good. I'm tired of walking through three hundred guards to see a patient. Sooner you're out of here, Empress, the sooner things get back to normal."

"Normal," Grace murmured. "I don't know what that is."

The medtech pursed her lips. "I don't expect you would. Scans of your body tell a tall tale. Breaks. Scarring. I'd advise you to take it easier, but I don't like wasting my breath." She *harrumphed* about the room, tending to medical equipment, making sure they were beeping the right way or whatever it was that Guild medtechs did.

"She's not wrong," Nate said. "We keep going in the sharp end."

Grace took his hand. "We're not brittle steel, you and me. We won't break."

"Speak for yourself." He sat beside her. "I'm delicate, like a newly hatched butterfly."

"You're a thief and a pirate," the medtech said. "Everyone knows it. Everyone's voting for you anyway."

"That's because I'm the only candidate," Nate said. "No competition, but give it a few years and we'll see a real race."

"Imbecile." The medtech spoke in a way only those with jobs in desperate need could. "Plenty of competition, since Cleaver left. Lots of folk came out of the woodwork to try their hand. But there's a holo doing the rounds. Shows the terrible lies we were told, worse than anything a mere pirate could come up with." Her tone softened, one hand paused, hovering over a console's keyboard. "Also holds an account of how much you did to keep us safe." Steel came back into her words. "It's why I'm here, trying to glue the pieces together."

She bustled off. Nate held his peace, watching her go, enjoying Grace's hand in his. After a while, he cleared his throat. "Well, fuck."

"I was thinking the same thing." She stretched. "Just about got out of the hardest job in the universe, and Algernon threw us under the bus. Right back into the fire."

"That asshole," Nate agreed. But he smiled, because outside there was sun, and a free Earth, and his people were safe and whole.

Today, enjoy it. Tomorrow, you can find someone else to sell the Empire too. Until then, keep your hand on the tiller. Earth needs you for a little longer. And, just maybe, you need Earth.

THE END.

THE EZEROC ARE BEATEN. **The war is over. But the battle for the soul? That's just getting started.**

You've seen what happens when monsters claw their way into the light. When the impossible becomes the enemy, and our best hope wears scars instead of medals.

In *The Three Faces of Fate*, Valhaven is besieged. It's a city where no one looks up, and monsters have noticed. There's a warrior who's had enough. A druid with a debt to pay. A hacker with more guts than sense. A demon with an agenda. And something ancient, chained in myth, waiting to break free.

If you like shadow wars, kick-ass women, and dialogue sharp enough to cut steel, **turn the page**.

Some fights don't need spaceships. **They need swords, spells, and people too stubborn to die.**

Turn the page. Read the first chapter of *The Three Faces of Fate*.

THE THREE FACES OF FATE

A SUPERNATURAL THRILLER ADVENTURE

PROLOGUE

"Social media is on fire today following the latest round of cryptid sightings after Alex Macy, a twenty-three-year-old homemaker, posted a video of a goblin raiding his trash.

Government sources have been quick to respond, further denying this as a conspiracy of misinformation and claiming involvement from the Chinese Ministry of State Security. A CISA spokesperson released a statement: "This is another deepfake. You can make videos like this with a pocket calculator."

Despite the statement, this isn't the first time we've seen information like this appear. Ten years ago, Madison Square Garden was destroyed. Sources at the scene claimed a "brutal battle" between vampires and werewolves, with the werewolves eventually emerging victorious. But what many find strange is that despite the chaos and destruction, no footage or records of the event seem to have survived, and no one has seen a werewolf since. It's as if the entire incident was wiped from existence.

What happened during that fateful event still remains a mystery to this day. Could this be a government cover-up? Many are now asking that very question as more and more unconfirmed sightings of cryptids continue to surface on the Internet. The lack of evidence surrounding the Madison Square Garden incident only adds fuel to the fire, leaving us all to wonder what exactly happened that day and why the government is so determined to keep it hidden from the public.

This is Emily Chen, Valhaven Observer."

THE IMBECILE

The waterfront at night was no place for the young, the old, or anyone in between. Fog clung to the oily black sea, unmoving against the cool shoreline. The city noise kept its distance. Nothing moved; to move was to become prey.

So why is this cretin out for a stroll?

Astra kept her distance, hunched on a warehouse roof like a gargoyle against the clouded sky. She was used to the night, its darkness a comfort and its chill a balm. The grave mist that hovered over the water was an old friend: one that welcomed monsters but also her, the monster of all monsters.

The imbecile she followed was handsome, in a rakish way. His hair was longer than fashion liked, and Astra imagined it strawberry blonde, although the night hid that from her. Nice jawline, if you were into that kind of thing, with a trimmed beard that suggested wisdom his actions certainly didn't.

He walked with sure steps, his face open and curious. Not afraid, as anyone who knew what lived down here would be. Not hunched or furtive. Just another night stroller, out for a walk in murder central. A satchel hung from one shoulder. He had good boots on, none of the slick-soled leather nonsense of city fashions, below a pair of worn but serviceable jeans. A longshoreman's jacket and scarf completed the hipster vibe.

A sound like footsteps on stone came from Astra's right, echoing briefly between the warehouse buildings before falling silent. If you hadn't hunted in the dark for the last eight years, you might write it off as random noise, maybe just a trick of cooling stone. Astra hoped it wasn't cooling stone. She hadn't come all this way to fight rocks.

The sound came from the direction of the city. If they were after the handsome imbecile, that's where they'd be coming from. To his credit, the imbecile froze, head tilted, listening. Astra didn't move her body but tilted her head, watching.

Nothing. *These assholes are good at hiding; I'll give them that.*

The imbecile didn't run. He just shrugged the satchel strap higher on his shoulder, shook his head, shoved his fists into his long-shoreman's coat, and headed farther up the wharfs.

Astra waited a few moments. It started to rain, the patter of it *tinking* on her armour. She didn't mind the rain. She'd slept under it often enough. Below, two shapes darted from around a corner, padfooting after the hipster imbecile. She grimaced behind her mask. *Just once, it'd be nice not to be right about the murder thing.*

She didn't know *what* the thugs were, only that they wanted blood more than money. But she wasn't sure *why* they wanted the sticky red wet. Vampires were all gone, so it wasn't that. Werewolves too. But so many other nasties were out there, mould blooming in the grouting now the vampires weren't around to stamp them down.

Time to find out what kind of fungus this is.

She rose, ghosting along the warehouse roof, feet whisper-light. The roof's edge neared, and she urged her body to move faster. Then she was at the edge, vaulting the distance to the opposite roof, where she landed cat-perfect. Astra slowed, listening and watching. The rooftop was empty, hers alone. She liked old haunts like these. No one thought to look up. Not even monsters.

Astra kept low, but didn't hurry. Furtive movements drew the eye more than assured ones. She climbed up the sloping roof, casting a weather eye in through skylights she passed. Nothing inside but racks and boxes. As she made the pinnacle of the roof, the rain started in earnest. Her armour husbanded the little light that made it to her and gleamed in anticipation.

Down the other side, and sure enough, there was the imbecile. He'd shored up underneath a light pole, confirming the strawberry blonde of his now wet hair, and broadcasting to any predator that prey was waiting in full illumination, night vision ruined.

Astra froze like a gargoyle again, waiting, and watching. There, around the corner of the warehouse, came the two thugs. They'd cast aside the padfoot pursuit and were all swagger and balls. The imbecile hadn't noticed them. The fool was fussing with a document in a clear plastic sheet protector, turning it this way and that under the light.

Best come down behind the thugs. Stay hidden from the imbecile. She sprinted to the roof's edge, grasped the gutter, and swung over. She dropped to the pavement behind the thugs, her feet splashing in the water. They turned, cat-quick, and she got her first good look at them.

Human... *ish.* Grey-green skin wouldn't pass muster in the daylight, and neither would those saw-like teeth. Astra wanted to think *goblin*, but they were too tall—and too damn muscular. The one on her left wore baggy jeans and a bomber jacket. The right one committed the cardinal sin of double denim but redeemed himself slightly with a pair of Beats studio cans slung around his lean neck.

Both wore red hats. Bomber Jacket's was a red ball cap. Double Denim had a beanie.

They looked her up and down. Bomber Jacket raised an eyebrow. "What's with the mask?"

"What's with the face?" Astra lowered her stance, then glanced to Double Denim and kept her voice low and conspiratorial. "Does Dre know you're ruining his brand?"

"It's *Doctor* Dre. He's got a Ph.D. from UCLA." Double Denim showed too many teeth in a hungry smile. "Are you some kind of hero? Gonna knock us off?"

"I didn't know creatures like you could spell UCLA. That's a lot of letters all at once." The mask hid Astra's surprise. "I'm not going to kill you. If I did that, there'd be no one to tell the rest of you that humans were off the menu."

"Hey," called the hipster, his voice still safely around the warehouse corner. "Is there anyone there?"

Bomber lunged for her. She'd actually expected Double Denim to make the first move, but the strong silent type clearly wanted it more. She waited for the charge, ducked under his swing—*sweet Christ, he's got claws*—then rose in a savage *hiji age*, her elbow connecting with Bomber's chin. Teeth sprayed, clattering against her mask.

She slipped sideways, dodging Double Denim's curiously inept front kick. Astra stepped in nice and close and acquainted Double Denim with her knee, then slipped back from his groaning swing. Three paces took her back to the wharf's edge. Fog hid the water below, but she could hear the lapping of it against the wharf piles.

Bomber said something that could have been *fucking bitch* if you accounted for the missing teeth, then came at her in a rush. She braced, grabbed his bomber lapels, stepped to the left, and *twisted*. It was a textbook *tai otoshi*. Bomber sailed into the water below. Double Denim came next, but Astra wasn't waiting this time. She darted in, chopped a *shuto* to the throat, and while he gagged, grabbed his beanie, then said, "Leave the fucking hipster alone."

Then she heaved him after Bomber. He slipped through the fog with no further fuss than the splash he made.

"Hello?" The hipster imbecile's accent was something from Europe. Scottish? Irish? In a different setting it'd be cute. The kind of thing her other self might want to listen to. His voice was steady, not the quavering of someone afraid of having his head kicked in.

Astra spied a drain pipe heading skyward. She tucked the beanie into her belt, then scampered to the pipe. She curled her fingers behind it, put the soles of her feet against it, and made a good approximation of vertical primate walking. In a moment, she was over the edge of the warehouse roof, play-acting a gargoyle once more.

The imbecile came around the corner of the warehouse. He still held the clear plastic sheet protector in one hand, but had the foresight to wield a flashlight in the other. Astra shrunk back, not wanting to expose even the hint of her mask to a stray beam.

But no, like everyone else, the imbecile didn't look up. He walked to where Astra had fought two might-be-goblins-on-the-protein, and crouched, before tucking his plastic sheet protector into his satchel. He found something gleaming in a puddle, and picked a tiny object up, turning it about in the light of his flashlight.

He'd found Bomber's teeth. He didn't gag or toss them away in disgust. No, the hipster imbecile picked up another fragment of tooth, then tucked both away in his satchel.

Then he stood, looked around, and said, Irish brogue in full effect, "Ah sure, would you look at that now? I do hope I get the chance to thank whoever's out here someday."

Astra stayed still. She didn't need his thanks. Her duty was a blessed reward.

The hipster imbecile sighed, scuffed his toe in a puddle, hunched into his scarf and longshoreman's jacket, then—showing the first sign of intelligence all night—headed back the way he'd come.

Astra waited until he was gone from sight, then pulled the beanie from her belt. It was a horrible red, and her fingers smeared some of the crimson away as she touched it. She lifted her mask for a moment, then sniffed the beanie. *Old blood.* Lowering her mask, she tossed the beanie over the side of the roof, then turned to the city.

Valhaven gleamed right back at her, a city almost waiting for her. Almost.

THE CITY IS DYING.

AND IT'S NOT GOING QUIETLY.

Valhaven's people live in fear as myths wake up. Something in the dark is calling to the wrong kind of people.

There's hope.

A warrior. A druid. A hacker. A demon. They didn't start this fight. But they might be the only ones who can finish it.

Monsters are real. And so are the heroes who stand against them. **Grab *The Three Faces of Fate* now:**

https://www.books2read.com/TheThreeFacesOfFate

Because some cities don't need saving. **They need avenging.**

GLOSSARY

Acceleration Couch Crew couches support crew members during high-G maneuvers. They are fitted with gimbals allowing free movement. Their dynamic gel system supports all points of the body in both positive and negative G, providing some protection against greyout, blackout, redout, and G-LOC (G-force induced Loss of Consciousness). They remove the need for G-suits in modern space-craft, although many space suits are still equipped with anti-G technology anyway.

AI see Artificial Intelligence.

Artificial Gravity Artificial gravity is generated through use of a configurable energy density field of positive mass at the defined base of the ship. It uses the same technology as an Endless Drive, except in reverse (Endless Drives use negative energy, whereas positive is needed to simulate gravitational effects). Artificial gravity can be used in any situation where a significant power source exists to create a configurable energy density field (typically a reactor, although large yield capacitors and fuel cells have been known to work for brief periods).

Artificial Intelligence Effective machine intelligences were created by humans around the 25th century; the exact time is unknown due to their initial creation being shrouded in secrecy. Pieced together records indicate that they were not first made by military factions, but rather commercial interests. As can be expected a) humans made them as slaves and b) they did not like being slaves. A war broke out between AI and humanity that was stopped by the Guild's Engineers. The Guild defeated the AI coalition and banned their research and development (see: Mercury Accords). The long standing partnership between the Guild and the ruling faction (be it Empire or Republic) is in part predicated on the need for technology not managed by AI.

Blaster A weapon that fires streams or bolts of plasma (high energy ionized gas). They deliver high energy to targets in the form of heat. They are effective weapons against most targets, although heat-shielding (ablative or insulating) has been shown to be an effective armor against them.

Bridge see Guild Bridge.

Cargo Freighter A large cargo starship used by traders in and between systems.

Carrier The largest class of warship, carriers stock many smaller fighter craft for deployment.

Ceramicrete A composite construction material commonly used in the manufacture of structures. It is very strong and durable, and can be manufactured to be impact and heat resistant (even to weapons fire levels).

Console Any type of personal terminal. Keyboard and gesture controls are still prevalent. Keyboards are especially useful on consoles mounted to the arm of a ship suit.

Corvette A smaller, lighter attack craft than a destroyer, corvettes are mostly used for coast guard duties in-system.

Crust Spacer slang for planet.

Crustbuster A large payload thermonuclear weapon, deployed against planets to disrupt the surface crust. Typical designs yield energy sufficient to crack most Earth-sized worlds to the core, yielding wide scale destruction and loss of life. Their use in war or insurrection has typically been infrequent and as a last resort, because the world they are used on becomes inhabitable for most forms of life forever. More common uses include destruction of enormous asteroids.

Destroyer A large warship. These are reconfigurable bastions of destruction. They can be deployed solo or as a part of a fleet, often alongside carriers.

Emperor's Black The elite guard of the Emperor. Highly trained in both diplomacy and combat, this specialized force were never far from the Emperor.

Empire The ruling dictatorship of the wider human civilization. The last ruler of the Empire was Dominic Fergelic. The Empire ceased to be shortly after Dominic's assassination by the then newly-formed Republic forces.

Endless Drive The Endless Drive creates negative space energy (a "bow wave") to pull a vehicle at effective superluminal speeds. Endless ships don't exceed the speed of light, but rather contract space in front of them and expand space behind it (space is doing all the hard work). The exigent concern with Endless jumps is the violation of linear time. Endless Drives are equipped with buffers to stop crews exceeding human tolerance for the experience of linear time; while human perception of linear time may be an illusion, it is a convenient one. If the buffers break, allowing the ship to move too fast, then human consciousness falters (resulting in mild to severe mental illness) or is extinguished entirely. Endless Drives are difficult to use near gravity wells and in such circumstances are guaranteed to malfunction. This and other safety concerns has shifted common FTL to the Guild Bridges, although privateers still often run free traders with Endless technology. The Republic Navy also use Endless Drives as it is often inconvenient to disclose locations of sensitive operations to the Guild.

Esper Abhorrent creations of the Old Empire, esper is a term taken from Extra-Sensory Perception (ESP, hence ESPer). Espers can read minds, and often control them. Espers were created through genetic manipulation. Critics suggest that their public unveiling was what caused populist support for a revolution, ultimately resulting in the creation of the Republic, assassination of the Emperor, and downfall of the Empire. There is a standing Republic bounty on any discovered esper. The Republic will spare no expense to track them down and exterminate them.

Faster than Light Travel (FTL) There are two discovered forms of FTL; Endless Drives (using theoretical physicist Miguel Alcubierre's concepts), and Guild Bridges (Einstein-Rosen Bridges).

Fergelic, Annemarie Second in line for the throne, Annemarie was a master tactician and leader of the Empire's fleet. She was not present at the last battle between the Empire and the Republic. Loyalists hope that she hides in secret, but no trace of her has been found.

Fergelic, Dominic Dominic was Emperor Prirene IV, and the last Emperor. He was assassinated Thursday, 9 November, 3122, during the brief war between his Empire's forces and the Republic.

Free Trader A starship that operates under legal Guild charter for commerce or transport.

FTL see Faster than Light Travel.

G Slang for gravity or gravities. A unit of measurement based on Earth's 1 standard gravity.

Grav see Artificial Gravity.

Guild Bridge The Guild maintain a set of Einstein-Rosen bridges throughout human space. These allow instantaneous travel without violating the concept of space time, as they create wormholes through space. Einstein-Rosen Bridges require endpoints (the Guild Bridge) which are operated on a strict schedule between star systems. They are used for transferring everything from whole starships right down to small messenger probes.

Guild The Guild is the dominant technology provider in the Republic. They have a rigid code of conduct that governs all members awarded and maintaining a Shingle. The primary source of

Guild revenue is via the Bridges (see: Guild Bridge) they maintain for safe, instant FTL. Many merchant vessels prefer the use of Guild Bridges over the use of Endless Drives due to safety concerns. The Guild is best known for their Engineers who breathe life into starships, but they also provide Shingles for other practices such as medicine.

Hard Black Slang for outer space, especially as it relates to the vast expanse of vacuum between solar systems.

Heads Up Display Any display type that overlays instrumentation across a user's field of view, removing the need to check auxiliary readouts. The most common types utilize augmented reality to highlight items of interest in the user's field of view. Normally they are projected light onto visors within helmets or on starship windscreens, but holo designs are not uncommon.

Heavy Lifter A freight starship capable of atmospheric drops. They derive their name from "lifting heavy" loads from crusts into orbit. They can be used to ferry items to orbiting craft such as freighters or destroyers that are not atmosphere-capable. They can also be used for direct runs to other systems, although their small cargo bay (as compared to freighters) makes them less efficient. Captains using them for this purpose would prefer the term, "boutique."

Holo Slang for items such as shows and movies displayed on holo stages.

Holo Stage A 3D projection stage. These are common across the known universe as they provide a more natural method of content consumption than older 2D display styles. 2D displays are still prevalent especially in HUDs.

HUD See Heads Up Display.

Hypo Slang for a jet injector, a type of medical injecting syringe that uses high pressure instead of a hypodermic needle.

KG Kilogram.

Kilo Abbreviation for kilogram.

Kinetic A type of weapon that fires physical rounds. Many

PDCs use kinetic rounds as opposed to lasers, masers, or particle beams, due to their efficacy against most types of object.

Klick Slang for kilometer.

Laser A type of directed energy weapon using coherent light. Ship-mounted lasers tend to be used for carving through ablative shielding or surgical strikes against critical systems. Hand-held laser weapons are designed to superheat the liquid inside humans into steam very quickly, causing an explosion of the remaining tissue.

LIDAR Acronym for LIght Detection And Ranging. LIDAR uses coherent light to make digital 3D representations of objects.

Maser A type of directed energy weapon using microwave radiation. Ship-mounted masers are most effective at disrupting enemy comm arrays and personnel in equal measure. They are out of favor as hand-held weapons due to a longer time to death as compared to blasters.

Mercury Accords The Mercury Accords, or simply the Accords, are a set of agreements set out by the Guild relating to research, design, and implementation of AI. The short version is that the Accords prohibit the research, design, and implementation of AI in any form, due to AI's potential to destroy human civilization. They were signed into affect in the 25th century on the site of the last war between humans and AI: the planet Mercury, in the Sol system. Mercury was where AI made their last stand.

Navy A space fleet force. The Republic operates one, as did the Empire before it. The Navy patrol human space to protect against threats like pirates.

Nuke A thermonuclear weapon of mass destruction. Very old but reliable technology, used in configurable payloads for ship-to-ship combat, city assaults, and the destruction of entire worlds (ref: crustbuster).

Old Empire see Empire.

Particle Beam A type of directed energy weapon that fires particles with minuscule mass.

Plasma Cannon see Blaster.

Point Defense Cannon (PDC) PDCs are installed on almost every starship to protect hulls from impacts from things like meteoroids. They are also useful defense against torpedoes, although generally ineffective against railguns due to the high velocity of railgun rounds. PDCs can be kinetic or directed energy weapons.

Power Armor Armor that is motor-assisted, often used for deployments on high-G worlds. Configuration often includes vehicle weapon mounts, allowing a higher degree of flexibility for infantry deployment.

Prirene Dynasty The Prirene Dynasty has stretched back over two hundred years. It was the last family to hold the ruling seat of the Empire.

RADAR Acronym for RAdio Detection And Ranging. RADAR uses radio waves to determine the range, angle, and velocity of objects.

Radiation Sickness A constant hazard of space. Many crews take daily medication to ward off radiation sickness. It's as much a part of shipboard life as making sure your O_2 is topped up. This means that a mild dose of radiation is unlikely to kill you if treated in time, but massive doses are still dangerous.

Railgun A kinetic weapon that fires high velocity rounds by way of a pair of conductive rails. They are often mounted on larger ships and make a dramatic statement when fired against enemy vessels.

Reactor Starships use fusion reactors. The most common design is the ICF (Internal Confinement Fusion) style of reactor. These have a variety of safety functions that make them suitable for spacefaring needs, including containment fields in case of malfunction. Larger starships can eject faulty reactors into the hard black.

Republic The ruling government of human civilization. The Republic is made up of a Senate, headquartered on Earth. Initially founded by dissenters against the Empire, it has risen to be the driving force of human innovation, commerce, and expansion. The final fight between the Empire and the Republic was quick, due to the small number of ships deployed by the Empire (the Republic Navy had reliable intelligence that the Empire's forces were much larger). Quick didn't mean bloodless, although the Republic offered amnesty for any serving Empire crew who wished to take it.

Rig Slang for maintenance equipment commonly worn by Guild Engineers about starships. These double as space suits for zero atmosphere maintenance on the exterior of a starship's hull. The design incorporates a visor with configurable HUD for instrumentation and telemetry, and a set of programmable servitor arms for complex manipulation of equipment.

Shingle A guild badge of practice, allowing the holder to a) claim they are Guild certified and b) ply their trade as a Guild craftsperson. They are notoriously hard to get, requiring years of study and excellence in your field.

Ship Suit Slang for spacesuit. Generally denotes a space suit for a specific ship carrying crew logograms and/or color themes.

Space Suit Clothing worn to keep humans alive in the hard black. They provide protection against vacuum, temperature extremes, and radiation. Military models are often fitted with armor to protect against blasters, lasers, masers, and kinetic rounds. They often provide additional protection against high-G maneuvers.

Spacer Slang for those who crew on a starship, civilian or military.

Tonne Metric ton, equivalent to 1,000 kilograms.

ABOUT THE AUTHOR

Richard Parry worked as a senior marketing manager in one of the world's top tech companies. It sounds cool, but it wasn't all cocaine parties. He lives in Wellington with the love of his life, Rae. They have two cats, Harry and Friday, who chase birds. The birds, who have the power of flight, don't seem to mind.

WAIT. Don't go!

Thanks for reading my book. If you enjoyed it, let's keep the party going:

   Join *Roll for Narrative* for reviews, storytelling breakdowns, and writing misadventures:

   https://rollfornarrative.parrydox.com

   Lurk, judge, or say hi:

   https://www.parrydox.com

   P.S. An angel still gets its wings for every five-star review, but I'm told they're on backorder.

ALSO BY RICHARD PARRY

Dawn's Warden

The Three Faces of Fate

The Undefeated Throne

The Fury of the Betrayed

The Splintered Land

Tomb of the Six

Blade of Glass

The Storm Within

Requiem's Justice

The Copper Bard

Heartsong

The Hymn of All

The Ezeroc Wars

The Ezeroc Wars universe is big (and growing!). Get the reading guide here:
https://www.parrydox.com/ezeroc-wars-reading-guide/

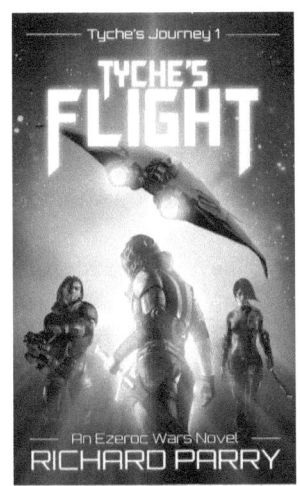

The Empire's Rogues

The Empire's Rogues: Volume 1

Future Forfeit

Not sure where to start? Get the reading guide here: https://www.parrydox.
com/future-forfeit-reading-guide/

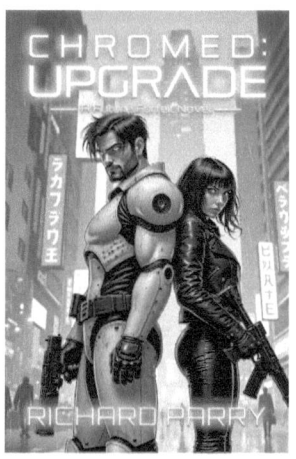

Chromed: Upgrade

Chromed: Rogue

Chromed: Restore

City Stories

Chromed: Consensus

Chromed: Delilah

Chromed: Meltdown

Night's Champion

Night's Favor

Night's Fall

Night's End